AN UNNAMED PRESS BOOK

Copyright © 2020 Jessica Gross

All rights reserved, including the right to reproduce this book or portions thereof in any form whatsoever. Permissions inquiries may be directed to info@unnamedpress.com. Published in North America by the Unnamed Press.

www.unnamedpress.com

Unnamed Press, and the colophon, are registered trademarks of Unnamed Media LLC.

ISBN: 978-1951213121
eISBN: 978-1951213138

Library of Congress Control Number available upon request.

Cover Art by Xiao Wang

Designed and Typeset by Jaya Nicely
Manufactured in the United States of America by Versa Press, Inc.
Distributed by Publishers Group West

First Edition

HYSTERIA

a novel

JESSICA GROSS

The Unnamed Press
Los Angeles, CA

For my parents

and my analyst

HYSTERIA

Chapter 1

I had come so many times staring at the latticework of my radiator that I wondered if I could orgasm from that pattern alone. It was the first thing I saw when I blinked myself into the room: those interlocking carved shapes. There, if I squinted, were the hot bars of its center. And there was the old wooden dresser, which my parents had sent off with me, and the streaked mirror propped on top. My cheap curtains looked ethereal in this particular slant of light, gauzy and white. Beyond it, the slender window opened out onto the roof: no breeze.

Blood pressed against the underside of my skull. I pictured the top of it lifting off and shooting into the air, a geyser of blood propelling it up into the clouds; then, in the remaining bowl of my head, my naked brain, sad and lonely. I shifted onto my back, stared at the spinning ceiling, peeling paint, and took inventory, as I did the moment each day I released sleep and reentered an existence on earth. On a rare day, I could scour the day before and discover that I had nothing to repent for. The images came in flashes: the face of my student, dilated with fear—she had fallen asleep at her desk, *how dare she,* and I'd rapped the desk right next to her ear, shocking her awake; then, the acidic rush of shame—an uptown bar, happy hour after school, cracked leather, broken jukebox, peanut shells coating the floor—two margaritas? three? the lips of the glasses caked in salt—and then the Indian restaurant downtown, holiday lights blaring from every wall though it was autumn, handle of vodka and bottle of cheap red wine in the center of the table—and, afterward, the party. I had said I wouldn't sleep with him. He was my roommate's brother: off-limits. He would walk me home, I had decided, and then I'd say goodbye. I touched the insides of my thighs, where the points of his hips had rammed into me, likely leaving me bruised. Yes, the events of yesterday would need to be repented for. Today I would be good. I would lock myself up if I had to.

My phone pinged. I reached for it on the floor. It was an email from my mother: "Dinner." My anxiety whooshed into flame, as it did every Saturday, when I agonized over whether to attend. When I was in middle school, my parents had switched from date nights out to hosting dinners in our apartment, and had kept up the tradition for the past decade, more or less. For a time, their friends' children had come, but one by one they'd grown up, and now there was just me. I'd forgone a party with my teacher colleagues to attend the weekend before, when my parents' guests had included a new associate, a Dr. Langham, a tree trunk of a man with a thick black mustache. He had recently gotten divorced, falling from virtuous expert to failed husband. I wondered if my parents had invited him as a show of magnanimity. It felt to me like an alignment: we were two unbelongings.

In the middle of dinner, during a tense conversation about borderline personality disorder, I'd taken a prolonged break in the bathroom. When I came out, Langham was perusing the bookcase outside my parents' bedroom. We had been seated across from each other at the table and had been flicking our eyes at each other all night. His shoulders were broad as a woolly mammoth's beneath his blazer. His face had grown meaty with age, he looked older than my father, but I could still make out the handsome bone structure underneath. I walked over and turned toward the bookshelves, too.

"Rough crowd," he said.

"Right?" I said, and then felt embarrassed. I tried again: "I'm sorry about your divorce."

"Thank you," he said, and turned his face toward mine.

My throat tightened, and I found myself unable to look in his direction. Was it his shoulders, the heat emanating from his heft, the shadow of his body on the bookcase, the memory of us glancing at each other across the table? I stared at the books instead: there, to the left, was the volume in which I had investigated, as a child, the disorder of one of my father's clients. My parents had often spoken of their clients in front of me, referring to them with code names, as if they were spies on a mission. I sat still in these moments, not daring to move for fear they'd remember I was there and stop speaking. This particular woman—Client Z was her code name—had graduated from college not long before and was bulimic. One day, when my parents were both working in their office, the apartment next door to ours, I'd taken down a psychology book to look up what this meant. *Boo-lee-mick, boo-li-mick, bu-lee-mick.* It meant that Client Z ate a lot of food, then made herself throw it back up, over and over again. This was disgusting and fascinating to me, and I knew at once that it was the thin, pale woman with oily black hair curtaining her face. I'd seen her through the peephole. I remembered, looking at the bookcase, how she'd walked with a hunch, staring at the floor. I'd gotten a glimpse of her face, one afternoon; I'd stood on tiptoes at the peephole for long minutes near the time I knew her session was to end, gaze glued to the hallway, determined not to miss the moment she passed by. She looked splotchy, like she'd been crying. I'd pictured my father putting his hand on Z's cheek, wiping the soft pad underneath her eye with his thumb, her tilting her cheek into his palm, closing her eyes.

Langham had shifted beside me, bringing me back into the room. It was the secret-in-public, perhaps, that I had responded to—like a laser beam, piercing through the cloud of table conversation, visible only to Langham and me. "He's on week four of his shame-attacking exercises..." Langham's eyes. "Did you read the new paper on..." Langham's mustache, his lips. "I heard she sold the practice!" Langham's large fingers, curled around his fork, which he sank into the pillow of his potatoes. That had sealed it, somehow: his hand on the fork. And then, as we stood at the bookcase, finally beside one another, my parents were one room away as tension built thick between us. I sensed his head rotate away again. But he was there, I knew I could have him, and this was enough to make me wet. I sank into this dependable sensation: escape, certainty, home.

The *DSM*-5 was right in front of my face, flanked by a biography of Truman and a thick volume on the history of the zipper. Langham reached toward the zipper book, his arm brushing my shoulder. He flipped to the back.

"How could anyone possibly read six hundred eighty-three pages on the history of the *zipper*?" he asked.

We both laughed, and this dispelled my paralysis so I could turn toward him. I let myself linger on his face. His mustache, though thick, was trim and well combed, and the skin of his cheeks looked soft, like he'd just shaved. I wondered what his aftershave smelled like. The hum of conversation wafted from the dining room. He took a small step toward me, as if to give me room to retreat. Scent of cedar. His eyes moved over my face, taking in its details, too; I wondered if he approved of my eyes or found fault with my nose. We were negotiating a kiss, informing each other that it was on the horizon. I held his gaze. I willed him to pursue me, the ultimate control. He leaned in, his mustache scratching my face.

Since that night last week, every time the phone rang my heart had jumped in excited panic. But it was the drugstore, a wrong number, my roommate asking me to buy toilet paper—never my parents, having discovered Langham and I had fucked in my father's walk-in closet, calling to confront me. Once, it was Langham himself, but I hadn't picked up, and he hadn't tried again. I wasn't sure how I expected my parents to make the discovery, just that they would. But I'd been left only with a searing image of Langham's hairy round belly pushing up against mine.

I hovered a thumb over my phone. My hand was trembling as I swiped down then up, bringing the word "Dinner" on the home screen into and out of view. My heart clunked against my rib cage as if trying to escape. *We know what you did.* I couldn't open it yet. I tossed the phone away from me onto the bed—*calm down*—and reached my hand between my legs. Images flooded me: A hand on my throat. A stingray. My head, yanked back by the hair. Twin orbs of a man's ass, thick eyebrows, a swish of black hair, fingers digging into my flesh. I never came when I was with a man—I hadn't last night—but alone, I could be the animal I was.

Afterward, I pulled on jeans and slipped my phone into the back pocket.

Downstairs in the living room, my roommate was sitting on the couch reading a magazine, her long legs curled under her. Her flushed cheek was still etched with the crosshatched pattern of her blanket.

"Morning," I said, and she smiled sleepily and stuck one leg across the couch, rubbed the cushion with her foot. Her feet were long and delicate, like greyhounds. I could feel the email boring into my skin through the denim, a spot of heat. I slid my phone out of my pocket and put it on the little table next to the couch and sat beside her.

Jojo looked like a catalog model, even in her thin gray sweatpants, fringed at the bottom where she'd cut off the elastic. Women instinctively touched their boyfriends when she passed. She had been three years ahead of me in college; her previous roommate had left to move in with her boyfriend, and I'd found the apartment over the summer through the alumni email list. My toes were close to Jojo's thigh and I wanted to wedge them underneath. She tossed her magazine on the side table and stretched her arms up with a little squeal, her shirt inching up her stomach, the tiny blond hairs there glistening like fine tinsel.

The waistband of her sweatpants stretched between her hipbones. She asked me what had happened with Sam.

Her brother. An image of his wide-open eyes last night, locked on mine as we fucked, surged into mental view. I winced and then, conscious of Jojo's gaze, coughed into my elbow.

"He went home late," I said.

"Oh," she said, extending the vowel and squinting at me. My stomach clenched.

"Nothing happened," I said, as casually as I could. I picked at a scab on my arm, then bent toward it, investigating it, absurdly. The Indian restaurant, his knee touching mine, the party, the kiss in the stairwell, the walk home, the moment outside our door. Jojo had left the party early, was already asleep. I had snuck him in—"Shh," I'd said, over and over, whether to him or to myself, I didn't know. "Why?" he'd said, too loudly, teasing me, but I'd only shaken my head, made my eyes wide to make him shut up, grabbed his hand and pulled him up toward my room, the why being, of course, that Jojo couldn't know. She couldn't *really* know—though the fantasy that she would, despite my having clamped Sam's hand over my mouth while he fucked me, had made me feel high.

Finally I looked up at Jojo, whose gaze ping-ponged between my two eyeballs, as if to figure out what I was hiding. In the few months we'd been living together, I'd tried never to bring my private life to the apartment, to always maintain the veneer. I didn't know how much she knew or suspected, and was always alert for signs she'd discovered the essential me under whatever illusion she was accustomed to seeing. At times, I was overcome by the conviction that although she was several years ahead of me in college, she must know my reputation—I imagined her whispering with her friends about me, telling them with wide, mischievous eyes what it was like to live with me. Yet usually I could talk myself out of these reveries, remind myself how little she'd seen, how little she probably knew.

But this time, I had misbehaved at home. And with Sam. Jojo's eyes were exactly the same as his, I noticed now—hazel, the pupil encircled by a ribbon of yellow. I'd been ravenous for as long as I could remember, but I had always managed, somehow, a bit of space between that life and the one I presented to those I knew. I'd fuck you in *your* home, not mine. I'd fuck you in a library, where only strangers could see us, or in a bathroom at a bar. I had never before slept with someone in my parents' house. I had never before slept with a roommate's brother. *Never again,* I'd sworn to myself as soon as he'd left, as I always did. *Tomorrow I'll start over.* But I would probably have to see him again, and what would happen then? I could move to a different apartment. Sam could decide to move to California, London, Australia. He could get hit by a truck—*I hope he does,* I thought, before I could stop myself.

"I mean, we made out a little," I blurted, then bit my tongue with my incisors.

"Well!" she said, in a way that made me afraid. Her tone pretended at lightness, but there was an undercurrent of censure. Or was it panic? Her facial expression was inscrutable. I played her exclamation over as I averted my eyes—*Well!* There was a world in which she was just happy, wasn't there, in which she detected nothing, in which she was even excited about the prospect of her brother and her roommate...

"He's great," I said.

"He is," she said, like a warning.

I wished I could rewind time, excise the experience, lay my head in Jojo's lap instead, curl my knees into my chest, have her pet my head, her piano-player fingers running through my hair. Did she know about me? Disgusting, for sleeping with Sam and for pushing him away, which I knew I would now do. Had to do.

My phone pinged on the table. I peered over at it. A text from my mother:

So?

Langham.

"What is it?" Jojo asked.

"Something from my mom," I said.

"Read it to me," she said. She came from a raucous midwestern family and found the dynamics of my own baffling and amusing. When she'd lost her first tooth, her brothers had paraded her around the house while her mother played a recorder and her dad clapped along. I tried to imagine my mother playing the recorder I'd brought home from school. I pictured her lifting it up off the living room table, holding it at arm's length, and peering at it with suspicion.

"I'll read it later," I said.

"Come on." Jojo jostled me with her knee. Read the email aloud? Reveal to Jojo what I'd done and, worse, my mother's disapproval? But, I realized, I could edit as I read, depending on how explicit my mother was—a possibility that gave me a shot of pleasure, electrifying as sex in a public park. And it would mean we'd stop talking about Sam. I reached for the phone and slid the screen open.

> Dinner tonight. We are gathering at 8p. Thomas and Patrice, our young new colleague Olivia, Richard Langham, and your aunt and uncle will be there. They are visiting for the weekend and they want to see you. You could wear the black pants. I am making the cassoulet. Your father is making his salad. 8p sharp. Will you be there?

That was all.

Jojo raised her eyebrows. "Do Jewish people have constipation because of their bodies or their anal-retentive personalities?"

I forced a laugh. The spot above my lip was radiating heat, like it always did when my body wanted to cry and I wouldn't let it. Whether they were tears of relief or anger, disappointment or sadness, I didn't know.

"I'm going to Celeste's party tonight," Jojo said, perceiving something. Celeste was one of her friends from college. "Want to come instead?"

The party should be safe; I'd met Celeste before and she had regarded me with what seemed like casual kindness, and I really didn't know many people from their year. I picked at the cuticle of my thumb, then stuck it in my mouth to chew off the dead skin. I could skip the dinner party, not see Langham again, not get the trapped feeling, almost terror, that enveloped me as soon as I stepped into our apartment—*my parents'* apartment—each time. But who was this "young new colleague"? Would she sit in my seat? What if my mom already knew she liked cassoulet and was making it specially? What if my dad laughed—at *her* joke?

The kitchen timer dinged.

"My waffles!" Jojo said, and bounded through the archway separating the living room from the kitchen. The timer was a kitschy thing she had found in a junk shop, and she used it as much as possible, even when unnecessary. It looked like an egg, with a plastic chick hatching from the top. His expression struck me as panicked: *I'm not ready to hatch!* I watched her bend over the waffle maker and lift the heavy metal lid, studied the topmost knot of her spine, peeking out above her shirt.

"*Perfect,*" she whispered. Then, to me: "I have more batter—want?"

I shook my head.

I mentally scanned the email again. Why had my parents invited Langham, I wondered, when they had just had him over last week? Usually there was a rotating cast of guests; was it possible they *did* know about us and were waiting until I arrived, to give us a private "talk," or a public one? Would they dare to chastise Langham in such a setting? I couldn't imagine. Which would be worse: my parents confronting me in front of their friends and colleagues, my aunt and uncle, and Langham himself— or sitting face-to-face with my parents, alone? Would they speak to me together, or would my mother speak to me on her own? My father wouldn't do it without her, I was almost certain. I could go to the party with Jojo, avoid any of these eventualities, hide out in my new life—yet if they did know, if they did want to confront me, wouldn't skipping dinner exacerbate whatever was to come? Or, worse, would it make them finally give up on me?

I was trapped.

My stomach hurt.

Luckily, I had someplace to be. For the past few weeks, since the school year had started, I'd been taking myself to a bar on Saturday afternoons to do my grading for the week. It was a bribe—grade a paper, take a few sips—and it made me feel like I had company. I liked my teacher-in-a-bar persona: diligent, but nonchalantly so. Plus, by the time I left, I was usually tipsy enough to deal with the evening. I'd left my backpack with my school stuff near the entrance to the living room, and I slid out the accordion folder full of papers and tucked it under my arm.

"I'm going out," I called to Jojo.

"Are you sure?" She peeked out of the kitchen and waved the spatula.

I told her I was and waved the folder in return.

"Okay. Let me know if you want to come tonight..."

"I will." I turned abruptly and then, as a corrective, blew her a kiss. It felt rigid and forced. If I were auditioning for "Easygoing Roommate," I wouldn't have gotten the part. So I grabbed my handbag and fled, through the door and down the stairs, past our landlady's yapping dogs and out into the morning.

One good thing about a bad hangover, like having the flu, is the immediacy. There's little room for preoccupation with what transpired last night, or what's going to happen tonight, or next month, or next year. All that dissolves in the face of the pleasurable hum of pain: that low-grade nausea blooming like algae in the gut, the cotton ache in the skull. Soft bird chirps are piercing, the sun slices right through the brain, each car horn is an assault. The rest is for later.

Unfortunately, my hangover wasn't that bad.

It was noon, early for a Saturday in this neighborhood. We lived a twenty-minute walk west of the park. Our neighborhood was row houses, tire shops, a few artisanal this-and-thats, the subway roaring overhead, the swampy green canal. Homey, or trying to be, with a strong under-taste of the industrial. It felt barren at its core.

I walked northeast, toward neighborhoods riper with life. A girl rode a plastic kid's bike she was too big for, her knees bucking up past her shoulders. But she pumped vigorously, her feet spinning at a rapid clip. The air hinted at cold. The trees were mostly still green, but a few browned leaves lay scattered on the cement. I hadn't put on a jacket but I probably should have, or at least a bra; my nipples were obvious and I crossed my arms tight, pressing the folder into my chest. I thought again about the student I'd reprimanded the day before—Lacey was her name. I had banged the desk right next to her face like some kind of dictator. The classroom was the one place I was usually able to keep my temper tethered, and I was never more ashamed than when it showed itself there. But today was not yesterday. Today I would atone. I stepped toward the curb to let the girl bike past me and smiled at her, but she was on a mission, and I felt a puff of wind as she left me behind.

Even if my parents didn't know, if I went, I would be trapped with Langham for hours, with the question of whether it would happen again. His round belly pushing its way through my legs, the small snarl of his orgasm. I had, finally, looked away from his stomach and to the right, toward my father's rows of shoes. There were his "house shoes," a pair of soft brown moccasins. He'd been replacing each old pair with the same brand and style since I was a child. I used to slip my feet into them every so often, in secret, enjoying even the cold, clammy feeling when he had recently taken them off. Just behind them, almost out of view, was a pair of immaculate black shoes, polished, the laces not yet twisted through the eyelets. I resented him for having bought new shoes, for continuing to buy and want and live now that I was no longer there, much as in childhood I had resented him, and my mother, too, for their clients next door, their dinners away, their friends, whole worlds that had nothing to do with me.

Well, now I had fucked Langham: an incursion. Worse than the possibility that it would happen again, maybe, was that he wouldn't want it to. That he, not I, would determine the end. He would see me and realize I was nothing.

Theoretically, I could stay home alone tonight, or transform myself into one of those "independent" young women who take themselves to dinner and a movie. But what would I do at the movies—sit seething with rage that everyone had someone but me? What would I do at home alone—masturbate myself into oblivion? I did think Celeste's party would be safe, but there was always the possibility I'd run into someone I'd fucked. It had been such relief, finally, to graduate, to stop trying to keep track of which classmates I'd slept with and where they would and wouldn't be, of where I would and wouldn't be met with a swirl of whispers, sidelong glances, reproachful glares. Jojo wouldn't invite Sam, at least I didn't think so. But how would my mother respond if I bailed? Would she whisper-yell—*selfish*—or, worse, would she be *just disappointed*, her voice grave? My father would withhold that across-the-room nod I often waited all night for—the nod that meant I had his attention and, more than that, his respect.

I looked up: there was the bodega and the auto body repair shop and the just-now-opening burrito place with its two tables behind a filmy window. The walls were painted yellow; the tables, bright green: a restaurant would be hard-pressed to choose a more nauseating color combination. The air had warmed, or maybe it was just my brisk pace. There was a creased sticky note on the sidewalk that looked poignant. "Meet S at—"

Pilz Bar was just around the corner. It was my favorite bar, with a dank interior perfect for making trouble you could forget about the next day. Even midday, the curtains were drawn, and when I walked inside it took my eyes a moment to adjust to the familiar space: the U of the bar with its heavy leather-topped stools, the bowl-shaped lights throwing dim orange circles, the banquettes along the wall. An Etta James song was playing, scratchy, like a digital recording overlaid with turntable static. If I squinted the smartphones' blue glare away, it felt as though it was a different era, and I was some sort of debauched scholar. Someone glamorous.

I stood at the bar, waiting. I'd come here enough that I was certain I knew all the bartenders, and I definitely knew Ed, who was laughing (fake) as he pulled a pint for a girl in overalls and a crop top, the bare skin of her sides peeking out in triangles, her voice lilting at him ridiculously. Farther down the bar was a second bartender, no one I'd ever seen here before. He had a thick beard, impeccably groomed, and eyebrows that matched. And then there were his eyes, which were narrowed slightly, as though he were in deep concentration. They were dark, and there was a warmth to them, but also a sense of reproach. *There is nowhere to hide,* said his eyes, and I was grateful they were not pointed at me.

I turned instead toward Ed, who greeted me with a wide smile. I knew it was his job to be pleased by my arrival, to make me feel at home. But it worked; I wanted his care and needed it.

"Dark and Stormy," I said, and he winked. Ed's drinks were watery concoctions, really not good. But he was one sturdy post in the world, and so I drank them.

I looked back toward the other bartender. There was a stern, set quality to his jaw. He wore the bar's regulation black T-shirt, a blue-checked towel slung over one shoulder, and I watched him reach for it to wipe the wet circles off the bar. There was an arrogance to his manner: he moved with deliberation, rushing for no one. Watching him, I could not shake the suspicion that I had seen him before, though I was certain I'd never seen him here. Did he simply remind me of someone? Had I seen him walking around the neighborhood or working another job? Or had I been examining his eyes with such ferocity that I'd become convinced I'd always known them? I couldn't believe the other patrons could stand his electric gaze. Lines of muscle flexed beneath the dark hair of his forearms. He had his left arm braced against the counter as he wiped with his right. I imagined it braced against a headboard.

Sam.

Jojo.

Langham.

My parents.

Dinner.

I closed my eyes and gave a brisk shake of my head, trying to loose the thoughts from my brain. If only they would unlatch like dandelion seeds, fly off in the breeze, leave my mind a plucked white bulb.

Ed slid my drink in front of me. *"Madam,"* he said.

I took a sip. "You're good," I lied, then dipped into my bag for my wallet.

"On the house."

"Yeah?"

"You can pay for your next one."

"Thanks," I said. I glanced toward the other bartender, who was now pulling a pint, squinting over the taps. His familiarity, which I still couldn't place, had begun to unnerve and excite me. His eyes roamed over the patrons of the bar, examining them intensely. "There won't be a next one," I told Ed.

"Ri-i-ight," he said. I walked away and his laugh slid through the bar, enveloping me.

The back patio of the bar was a series of long picnic tables, fences thick with ivy. Potted plants rimmed the edges of the concrete floor; strings of lights were draped across, lit even though it was day. A little storage nook had been built into the left-hand side, where one length of fence overlapped the other; the mops and buckets stored there were almost hidden behind a series of small trees.

I scanned the space, steeped in wan autumn daylight. A few men sat on the tables themselves, their boot-clad feet on the benches, women hovering nearby, hands stuffed into pockets. I felt a twinge of panic, unable to locate a safe place to sit and grade—there was a free table right in the middle, but I wanted to look *casual*, not like I was showing off—but crossing toward me now was Dominic, whom I hadn't seen for at least a year, since college. It was almost unreal that he'd be here, yet this was Brooklyn, I was discovering: a graveyard come to life. We'd left things on a not-so-good note, I supposed I'd maybe blown him off, but he seemed to have forgotten all that or at least forgiven me, his face broken open with warmth. He was more attractive than I'd remembered, black hair sweeping down over his forehead. He walked toward me, confident, unhurried. I mirrored his expression, smiling, my face soft. I blinked long and slow. Quiet confidence, we were communicating something. *Fancy meeting you here, how about that, we've found each other again after all this time.*

I kept that expression on my face as he walked past me. He wasn't looking at me at all, he was looking toward another girl, one he was now kissing. He had his hand on her hip, she flitted her eyes up at him, she tipped her drink toward him, he took a sip through the straw and scrunched his nose, said something probably about how it was too sweet, she laughed and swatted him on the arm, he kissed her again. The hot lava of mortification bubbled up in me. Who in this bar had witnessed my foolish open face, my starved smile, like I wanted to consume him?

"Dominic!" I called, to prove I really did know him. He didn't hear. If anyone hadn't seen my initial rejection, they knew now. "Dominic!" I said, louder, frantic even, and this time he heard me and turned. On seeing me, his joyful expression dissolved.

"Hi," he said, eyes narrowed, and turned back toward the girl. She looked sidelong at me as he spoke to her.

I stood immobile. I forced myself to swallow, to blink, then raised my drink to my lips and pulled a mouthful through the straw. I plastered a calm, beatific expression on my face, looked out toward the patio's back fence, pretended I was thinking items of depth and nuance, rather than staving off tears. My fingertips pressed hard into the folder, as if for sustenance. I remembered the weeks we'd spent in college, talking late into the night on his dorm-room bed, him tracing my forearm with his nail, so lightly, up and down. He'd had me close my eyes and walked his fingers from the wrist up the tendon that emerged there, all the way into the crook of my elbow. "There," I'd say, when I thought he'd reached the ridge, but when I opened my eyes, he was always inches away from that margin of skin. After we'd finally slept together, I noticed, for the first time, that his gums showed when he laughed, like he was a scared animal. I noticed his arms were skinny and weak, like a rag doll's. I noticed that he was barely taller than me, that he had a birthmark on the tip of his nose I'd never seen before. His lips had been the softest I'd ever tasted, and until that night I had hungered for them, but afterward they felt far too soft, like they threatened to swallow me whole. All at once, he disgusted me, and I couldn't bear to return his calls, so I didn't. I saw him across campus a week or two later and changed direction to avoid crossing his path. I thought he hadn't seen me, but maybe he had. Anyway, he refused to talk to me after that, so it was really more like he had rejected me.

I retreated to a corner near the door to suck down the rest of the drink. It really was bad, but when I reached the bottom of the glass, I dug the straw between the ice cubes to get those final droplets. My limbs went limber, the muscles of my neck released, I closed my eyes and felt around the inside of my mouth with my tongue. There were my teeth, sturdy and dependable. There was the palate where my tongue lived, which it nestled against when it went to sleep at night. I drew the tip of my tongue down the ridge in the middle, then back again. I felt a gaze burning into me, but when I opened my eyes, there was no one staring.

I looked across the patio. I felt empty and forlorn. Dominic and his little girlfriend were gone, who knows where. There were two young guys with half-drunk pints, the glasses sudsy, at the table nearest me—but they were already eyeing a blandly pretty girl down the table. She was sitting with a slightly less attractive version of herself, whom she surely brought around with her as a point of comparison. In the back corner a rangy guy in faded jeans sat on top of a table with his friends, feet on the bench, cigarette hand hanging limply over his knee. A big, bumpy man-knee. That hand. That knee. I knew all knees must be the same, but only men's knees seemed to point downward in those sharp, seductive Vs. Torture to behold, delicious torture.

He brought the cigarette to his lips; I followed with my eyes, catching on the V of his white T-shirt, where the dark hair curled up toward the knobs of his collarbone. Together with the two points of his knees, they made a flock of birds, V and V and V—I was sure I'd never seen such a beautiful collarbone, yes, like wings. I wanted to fit my lips like a notch to each knob, flick my tongue between them; I wanted to press my tongue flat into that hollow; I wanted to feel him shiver. He'd blown smoke right into his buddy's face, I saw—the friend was trying not to cough, but his eyes were watering, and finally he coughed into the crook of his arm. The first guy, my guy, took another drag.

Be good, I told myself, *stay where you are.* But I couldn't bear to; my chest was so tight I knew if I didn't move toward him, I would crack into shards. *You're supposed to be grading,* I thought, but the prospect of hunching over papers while this man sat smoking only feet away was laughable, if not impossible. I pressed my tongue to my teeth again: no matter what happened, my teeth would be there. I stashed the folder in a corner behind a plant, then went over, my breath shallow and quick, suddenly uncertain how one was supposed to swing one's arms while one walked.

"Can I bum one?"

"'*Bum* one,'" he said. "What are you, from a potboiler detective novel?" But he tapped his pack against his knee—that knee—and slid one out for me, then cupped his hand around my mouth to light it.

I asked stupid questions to fill the silence: where he was from, how many siblings he had, what he did, where he lived. He answered in as few syllables as he could; he asked nothing in return. But his voice was deep and scratchy, like a burnt log. His collarbone, up close, those hairs curling toward it; his rib cage, grazing his T-shirt as he inhaled. Sitting on the table like that, his face was at eye level, his knee right at my hip. I cupped it with my palm.

He took his cigarette out of his mouth, holding it lightly between two long fingers, and looked me over. His eyes caught on my nipples: they were hard, practically poking through the cotton of my shirt. My hand was still on his knee, and I tightened my fingers around it, its contours pressing into my palm. He pressed back. Heat flared between my legs. If I couldn't crush my body against his, I might die.

He cocked his head toward the storage nook, a question. I nodded, too vigorously; he got up and ground his cigarette into the floor and I did the same. He walked toward the nook, and I followed.

Inside, I reached up to kiss him, but he swung me around to press my back against the fence. He was so tall, blocking out the sun. The wires of the fence pressed into my spine. He tasted like soot. I reached around his neck and wrenched him in, I wanted him so close I could disappear. I was getting wet—Sam, Dominic, Langham— *shut up, shut up*—I let go of his neck and reached under his arms, around his back, pulled him toward me with my fingernails. He ground his crotch into mine, the button pressing painfully against me. I said nothing, it hurt in a way I deserved and maybe liked, instead I tipped my head back, biting the inside of my cheek, and let him kiss my neck. Oh God! I pressed into the button as long as I could take it, then another second, then another—then finally shifted away, the pain having obliterated whatever else was in my mind, or was it the ecstasy?

He reached around to squeeze my ass, I pressed into his hand, his collarbone was right at eye level and I stood on tiptoes to suck its twin cherries. I circled my tongue around one, then the other, then back again. He didn't respond. I looked up at him and his expression was blank. He wondered what the fuck I was doing. I brushed my hand over his dick and found it stiffening in his jeans, so I sank to the floor. I undid his belt and fiddled with the button of his pants.

"Whoa, kid," he said, and laughed a little. "Someone's thirsty..."

Fuck him. He would like it. I ripped his button open and the zipper down. His dick was still half limp, but I threaded it through the slit of his boxers, took it into my mouth.

"Okay, chill, chill," he said, but he shimmied his pants and boxers down his legs until they lay scrunched at his ankles. I opened my lips over his cock, gulped it down. It started to swell; he thrust his hips, his dick hitting the back of my throat. I grabbed his hips and shoved him farther inside me. Sharp points of gravel pressed into my knees through my jeans. The broad planes of Sam's face. Dominic's raised eyebrows. Langham's belly. I looked up,

I was desperate for his eyes but all I saw was the bottom of his chin, his head was tilted back, his gaze directed up, away from me, his quickening breath not meant for me, it was his own private pleasure.

When it was over I ran my tongue along my teeth, that sourness that would take hours to leave. I wiped my cheeks on my sleeves. He blinked his drooping eyelids.

"Wait, are you *crying*?"

"No."

His eyes popped open. "I did *not* make you do that. Fuck. I didn't make you do *shit*. Why the *fuck* are you crying?"

"It's allergies," I snapped.

He wrenched his pants back up and skittered out of there. I stayed in the little nook, peering through the slats of the fence as he hurried his bewildered friends up and out of the bar.

Chapter 2

When I'd collected myself—pressed the heels of my hands deep into my eye sockets, brushed the gray film of dirt from my pants, breathed into the denouement that follows a cry, made sure the guy and his friends were really, really gone—I walked across the patio, head down. My face had splotches of heat, the skin around my eyes was swollen, and I didn't want anyone asking if I was okay. I grabbed the folder from the corner and made my way back inside to the bar.

"Can I get a Dark and Stormy?" I said, eyes downcast. When I looked up I saw with a start that it was the new bartender and had the urge to bolt, but he was already taking one of the steamy glasses from the rack and filling it from the ice bucket. *Leave*, my mind said, but I was immobile, rooted to the barstool. I prayed he wouldn't ask if I was okay, that it was dark enough inside that he might not be able to tell. What would I say? That I'd cried while giving a blow job? And why had I? Usually sex was exactly what I needed not to feel a thing. *Black Hole*, I'd often thought of those minutes—blissful nothing. Blow job: blankness. Fucking: precious void. Sometimes I began fantasizing about the next man while someone was still inside me, as if to cushion against the excruciating moment when we'd have to part. But this time it hadn't been enough. I was starving.

I watched his eyes follow his hands. He raised the glass, caterpillar eyebrows pulled together, examining it to make sure the ice was at the right level. He placed it on the counter and then looked up, startling me out of my privacy. His gaze was an X-ray, making me squirm. I wished he'd look away first, but he didn't, and when I couldn't stand it anymore I cleared my throat and looked down. He resumed his work, pouring in the ginger beer from high up. The ice cubes cracked and melted, then settled into the fizzy pool of soda, and he poured in the rum, the thick dark liquid hovering at the top of the glass like a thundercloud.

I peered back up at him, head still down so I could look away quick. He was refocused on the drink, swirling it with a red plastic stirrer, then sliding a lime onto the rim. Perhaps he'd sensed my discomfort and was doing me a favor by diverting his attention. I lingered on the contours of his face, his cheekbones, the thin line of his mouth. Where did I know him from? Thick eyebrows, those eyes, beard like brambles. I wondered how it would feel against my palm. Whether I could shove my fingers so far inside it they would disappear. What could I search online—"man beard thick eyebrows"? I'd get images of half the men in Brooklyn. But then something flickered in my mind, like when you're trying to call up where you've seen an actor and get a hint—a gesture or a line from a previous role: *You can't mean it, you can't!* He set my drink before me.

"You look like someone," I said. I squeezed the lime into the drink, stirred it with the straw. My movements were languid; if I acted like I didn't care, perhaps I could coax him into replying. But my hand was quivering.

"Seven," he said. He had an accent, I noticed, sharp sounds slicing through air.

I placed the bills on the counter with an extra dollar for tip.

"Who do you look like?" I whispered, half to myself. I wanted him to wedge his fingers underneath my skull, into the folds of my brain. I wanted him to climb into my mind and see what I was seeing, what I was half remembering; to see what was inside, or underneath. *Look at me again.*

He didn't respond, and I wasn't sure if he'd even heard me. Instead he took the change and turned away, to slice lemons. His hand on the knife was better than Langham's—just as large, but less meaty, more deft. He had choked up the handle of the knife, like you were supposed to, so his pointer finger and thumb pressed into the steel. A thin vein threaded along his pointer finger toward his square fingernail, his hand on the knife, slicing against the knuckles of his other hand. Those sturdy fingernails, those fingers. Sometimes, when I was sitting and reading, or just standing at the counter, my dad, feeling tender, would squeeze the back of my neck. It was always a surprise, his touch so unusual and unexpected I would sit frozen to make the contact last, to feel the heat of his hand on my skin—and maybe it was a surprise to him, too, because more often than not his grip would tighten until it hurt just a little bit, as if his own sweetness had caught him off guard—

And then the image thrust its way into my consciousness, like a plant breaking through soil, clear as I'd seen it as a child, plastered across the cover of the book. My parents were early in their careers as therapists and had invited their colleague Patrice Lyle over for a cocktail. They were always exchanging books and papers, then meeting to talk about them while I eavesdropped, or tried to—none of the theory made sense to me, the shop talk could be duller than my math class in school, but once in a while they'd share stories about their patients, and this was what I lived for.

I couldn't remember what Patrice said, only my father's rejoinder: "Well, no need to be *Freudian* about it!" I remembered him laughing, his eyebrows pushed up toward his hairline, a laugh that unsettled me, falling as it did in that frightening gap between pleasure and disdain. I was sitting in the corner of the couch, almost invisible, a book splayed open on my lap, though at best I had been tracing the shapes of the letters with my gaze. Patrice laughed and shrugged in response. I guessed she was trying to soften him. I felt pained and embarrassed for her, but envious, too: she had, after all, made him laugh, whatever kind of laugh it was.

"What's 'Freudian'?" I asked, to make myself known.

My mother explained that Freud had invented a kind of psychology a long time ago. "Like you?" I had asked, but my parents had shaken their heads, amused. No one believed his ideas anymore, they said; those theories had been disproven. "Neurosis is a high-class name for whining," my father said. The kind of psychology my parents practiced, they explained, was supported by data. Freud's kind gave people a cop-out, letting them talk themselves into oblivion. My father said studies had proven their mode of treatment worked best: "Sem-i-nal!" my mother replied in singsong. There was something in their tone that unsettled me—their certainty, maybe; their flippant dismissal; or maybe their unity.

"But who *was* he?" I said. "Why doesn't anyone believe him anymore?" I looked from one to the other—at Patrice, who had sat back in her seat and was picking lint off her pants, to leave the matter to my parents; at my mother, who was looking toward my father, deferring. My father stood and left the room, and I wasn't sure if he would come back, but a few moments later, he returned with the book in his hands and gave it to me. I held it in my lap; it was heavy and pressed the spine of the open book below it into my legs. My father tapped his large fingers on the cover.

"This is him," he said. "Freud."

And yes, there he was: the man in his three-piece suit, one hand on his hip, the other holding a cigar. He looked straight into the camera with what was almost a glare. Everything about his posture suggested power, supremacy, and I remembered staring so hard my eyes went dry.

The conversation had continued. I opened the book and tried to read it, but the words made no sense to me; besides, I was too overcome to focus. So I closed it again, traced the outline of his face with my finger, traced his body, traced his hand. The cigar. His coat. His eyes.

The book went back on the shelf. A few times in the years that followed, I would pull it down in moments of particular despair and hold it to my chest. After a while it was enough to simply envision his face. Tantruming in my room, sobbing in a curl on my bed, I would picture his penetrating eyes and think, *Freud would understand*. My parents had shunned him, so in the moments they also shunned me, I imagined us a team. Freud and I. Once I discovered masturbation, that had become folded into my ritual: after I'd sobbed for a bit, I would reach down into my underwear. It was soothing; the orgasm would put the seal on the catharsis of the experience. It returned me to myself. I recalled at once the Freud of these childhood fantasies, him looking straight into my eyes with his powerful, intimate glare. Him reaching around my head, lacing his hands through my hair, tightening his fist. Or, sometimes, putting me over his knee, spanking me—*bad girl*—all the while wrenching my head around with his hand so we never broke eye contact. *Freud, Freud, Freud,* like a mantra, *Freud would understand.*

And now, behold: here he was. Or someone who looked exactly like him. The bartender had finished with the lemons and was sliding glasses into the rack above us, the bulk of them tinkling like a wind chime. When he turned away, I could see the hair at the nape of his neck curled into a little point, as if it had snuggled into the divot there to take a rest, like a newborn animal. And then he turned back toward the bar, back toward me. Those lips. Those eyes. It was uncanny. *He's not Freud,* I told myself—but *Yes he is,* I thought at the same time. I watched him reach up, again and again, to lace the wine glasses on to the wooden rack, his large fingers delicate around the thin stems. I imagined him in that three-piece suit, the cigar in his hand—his hand in my hair—my body draped over his knee—

And then he looked at me, into me, and I went numb. Still, I stared back. It was excruciating, I could hardly stand it; it was thrilling, I couldn't look away. He pursed his lips, like he was thinking something that he wouldn't let himself say. *I am Freud.* He gave a sharp intake of breath, but no words followed.

"What?" I whispered.

"I saw you," he replied in a low voice.

My body went rigid. I tried to take a casual sip of the drink but sucked in too much and it went down my windpipe. When I finished coughing he was still looking at me. I wiped my lips with the back of my hand.

"Saw me what?" I said, though I knew.

He gestured toward a video screen nestled into the corner where the bar top met the cabinet. It projected, in a series of little black-and-white squares, portions of the bar and back patio that were hidden from his direct view. In the bottom right square, currently motionless and grave, was the area tucked behind the fence.

For several moments, I was an animal playing dead. Maybe if I showed no signs of life, he would move on to other prey.

Time expanded like pulled taffy. I combed over the situation. What had he seen? The camera looked down on the area from on high, it was in black and white. He would have watched two grainy figures walk into the little cove, seen them pressed together, the smaller reaching her arms up around the neck of the larger. He wouldn't have made out her standing on tiptoes, straining. He would have seen her kneel. He wouldn't have seen the man's dick was still half soft. He wouldn't have heard his words: *thirsty... thirsty...* He wouldn't have seen the girl look up, searching—or probably he would have. I looked away from the screen. He would have seen the man run away. He might have seen me crying, if he couldn't tell from my face.

"What's gross is that you watched," I said. "Not what I did."

His face softened unexpectedly. "Who said it was gross?" he said.

"You did," I said. But he shook his head.

"You did."

I tried to ride a wave of anger, I tried to exert control over myself, but something was melting and couldn't un-melt.

"Did you want to be seen?" he said quietly.

"No," I said, but tears had started streaming down my face. My body, always disobeying me. I darted my eyes around the bar. There was no one in earshot. Well, fuck it if there were, I thought. What did he mean, did I want to be seen? Did I *want* to be *seen*? I glared at him, jaw clenched, trying to make him take it back, but he seemed immune. He maintained that softened expression, didn't say a word.

"What do you mean?" I prodded. "What do you even mean?"

"Just what I said."

"No." I slid off the stool, grabbing my things. "No, I didn't *want* to be *seen*."

"Wait," he said.

I tried to summon the strength, or the confidence, or the anger, or the something, to leave anyway, walk out, never hear what he wanted me to wait for. But it wasn't there. Something in me needed to wait; something in me wanted to hear. So I stood.

He reached under the bar for a napkin, scribbled something on it, and pressed it into my hand.

I walked for several blocks, then turned down a street of brownstones and sank onto the bottom stair of a stoop. I'd shoved the napkin into my pocket, unread; I would wait as long as I could bear, to maintain the sense of infinite possibility. His name and number? A compliment: *You're beautiful*? Or would it be a threat? *Find another bar. I mean it. You're no longer welcome here.* I was exhausted and lowered my head between my knees like people do to stave off nausea. *I saw you.* When I lifted my head again, I kept my eyes closed, watching the beads of color move beneath my eyelids. They formed paintings, landscapes, worlds. *I saw you.* And then the screen went black. I opened my eyes and a man was edging around me up the staircase, jostling grocery bags.

"Sorry," I mumbled.

He pursed his lips, made a show of just how much he needed to jostle to edge around me. I didn't move. He didn't *own* this staircase. I waited until I heard the door close and lock behind him; but as soon as he was gone, the staircase held no more appeal. I took one final moment of gathering, then pushed myself back up to make my way home.

I saw you — again these words echoed through my mind. I tried to remember the tone in which he'd said them, but the words had taken on a celestial, disembodied air. He could have said them with great judgment or with great remove, I couldn't now recall. Did it even matter? Well, it mattered.

I walked slowly, dreading home. I fiddled with the napkin in my pocket. *Hi*, it might say, *I think I'm in love with you.* It was definitively cold out now, and I crossed

41

my bare arms tightly against it. I wanted to be held; I held myself. *It is true,* the note might say, *I am Freud.*

Had I wanted to be seen?

Finally I reached back into my pocket for the napkin and squinted at his script.

Come back.

Chapter 3

I walked for a long time, to the park and through it, mind burbling, so long that by the time I got home, Jojo was getting ready for her friend Celeste's party. She invited me again to come. I still hadn't made up my mind about my parents' dinner, I felt a sickening anxiety every time I considered it, so again I put off the decision. My mother's email lay in my inbox, needling at me. I tried to put it out of my mind. I wouldn't reply yet, I would go with Jojo, and I would leave open the possibility of stopping by dinner later.

We walked to the F in thick jackets and bare legs. I'd changed into a long gray cotton shirt with a deep neck and loose sleeves that went to my elbows; I was wearing it as a dress, though it barely covered me. At the last minute, I'd transferred the bartender's napkin to my jacket pocket; it was my talisman, and now I folded my fingers around it, pressed it into my palm. Celeste's party was early; she had somehow gotten it into her head, Jojo had told me, that early-evening parties were more "refined." As we waited on a corner for the light to change, a dog dropped into shitting position in front of us. His owner tugged his leash a little, to no effect, then looked at her nails, embarrassed. The dog was small, with wiry white fur and a pert black nose that glistened in the cold. I watched him shit, the brown curling and steaming on the sidewalk underneath his quivering butt, his face pulled into a wounded expression at the forced indignity of his position. I couldn't look away, my sadness on his behalf filled me with familiar warmth, I uniquely understood his vulnerability and held it for him.

"Don't watch!" Jojo said, giving me a shove.

"Why not?" I said. But I looked away.

Our subway station was aboveground, and we stood shivering on the platform. We should have worn pants; the thin layer of daytime warmth had dissipated now that it was night. I looked at Jojo, her jaw clenched, the muscles there giving off little tremors. Her legs were goosebumped. I wanted to wrap my arms around her. I went up to the side of the track, peering into the darkness. No train.

"Don't stand so close, didn't you read about that woman who got pushed onto the tracks last week and died?" Jojo said.

"Right," I said. I lingered for a moment more, hoping the train would come; I wanted to be the first to see its twin lights winking from far away. *My chariot,* I would think, as if I had summoned it, staring it in the eyes as they broadened into bright circles, bringing with them the dual smack of sound and wind. But the tracks remained desolate. I stepped back toward Jojo.

My phone buzzed: Sam.

Last night wuz fun.

Jojo had told me he had a habit of "ironically" using colloquial misspellings from the early 2000s. Into my mind flooded his goofy, too-wide smile, his eagerness, the way he'd possessively cupped the back of my arm with his hand. I cringed. It had been late when I'd asked him to leave, the sky already threading through with light. I was desperate that Jojo not find out—or maybe I just needed to be free of him, from his sweaty flesh pressing into my back, his arm draped over my side, straitjacketing me. I'd made up something about how I wasn't ready to just *sleep* together yet, that it would be mortifying for him to hear me mumble in my dreams—something that made me seem tender. Whatever: he had left. Another buzz. I looked at my phone: the kissing emoji, his mouth pursed into a farcical chicken beak, from which emerged a tiny floating red heart. One of the emoji's eyes was closed while the other remained open. I knew this was meant to be read as a wink, but to me the image resembled a spy, faking the abandon of a loving kiss to distract us while his one open eye, alert, roved around for his next mark.

"What?" Jojo said, arching over my phone.

"Nothing," I said, but she had seen it.

"'Last night *wuz* fun'! Aw, Sam. Tell him to come," she said, and then looked at me hard, like it was a challenge.

"Maybe," I said, and forced a smile.

"Why," she said, "you want to see who else is there?"

"No," I said, and I could feel my heart begin to race, "it's just that I might stop by Celeste's for only a little bit and then go to my parents' for dessert, and I wouldn't want to invite him and have him get there and then, you know, I'd already—"

"Okay!" she said, palms splayed. "Okay."

Sam texted again:

What are you up to tonight?

I slid the phone back into my jacket pocket. There was the napkin.

I saw you. I saw *you. I saw* you. How far down had he seen?

We transferred to the C at Jay Street and got out at Eighty-Sixth, right alongside Central Park. It was almost dark, thin black branches slicing into lavender. Jojo was hunched over her phone. I gazed toward the buildings facing Central Park: most were doorman buildings, their names stretching in script across their awnings. I had grown up in a building like that on the other side of the park and had an instinctive aversion to them now, those long awnings' promise of protection.

"Found it," Jojo huffed at her phone. She looked at me, then lightly slapped my cheek. "Are you there?"

"Yeah," I said. "I'm here."

A guy wearing spandex under his shorts ran past us, threads of muscle flexing in his pale, skinny calves. His face had a set, almost vacant expression, like he was freezing and miserable, malnourished and tired, but conscripted to run and run. He turned into the park and I watched his thin back, tilted forward toward the heart of the woods.

Jojo blew heat onto her hands, rubbed them together, the tips of her ears bright pink. "Let's do this," she said.

The building was a brownstone with a stoop, flanked by a fence wound with ivy. Even in the darkening night, I could tell it was fake, the papery green leaves linked by black wire—but if you looked quickly, it was picturesque, even dreamy. Celeste's apartment was on the fifth floor. We'd barely knocked when one of her friends opened the door. Benny. He had been in Jojo's year in college, but we'd taken a music class together; we'd fucked in one of the practice rooms after class one afternoon, underneath a piano. *Shit.* But this guy slept around, sex was nothing to him, he probably wouldn't have told anyone or cared, he was nothing like Dominic, it was okay. If it was just him, at least, it would be okay. I still remembered the sheen of that piano, how I'd pictured someone polishing the expensive wood each day, one arm reaching back and forth across the instrument. The party was already madness, a wall of hot air and sound bursting through the doorframe.

"Oh, *heyyyyy!*" Benny said, stretching his arms wide, ragged, holey T-shirt emblazoned with our college's name. Jojo gave a grand bow in greeting.

"Sir," she said. Her hair hung over the back of her head toward his feet, almost grazing his toes. She flipped her head back over, a cascade of burnished gold. He grinned, his mouth practically a boner. I moved between them, placed both hands on his shoulders.

"We come in peace," I said. I stared at him, telegraphing the memory of our joint reflection in the floor-length mirror, the piano guarding us, me on hands and knees, jolting forward over and over—

"I'm sure you do," he said, looking down and moving backward into the room. I felt sick, wanted to run back down the stairs and out into the darkness. I curled my fingers around the napkin. *Come back.* I could leave. *Do it.* But he held the door for us, and we walked inside.

Celeste was perched on the arm of her couch, her tiny body draped in a shimmery white sheath. She gestured grandly as she spoke, her subjects on the couch turned toward her, grinning like supplicants. She caught sight of us squeezing through the entrance hallway and bounded over. "I haven't seen you in a million years!" she trilled, gathering Jojo and me, by default, into a massive hug. I closed my eyes and let my head lean into Jojo's shoulder.

"It's been two weeks!" Jojo laughed, pulling back and breaking the circle.

"Two weeks too *long*." Celeste cupped Jojo's face in her hands to plant a kiss on her lips, then turned toward me. "Great to see you again," she said. "I'm glad you came." The formality of her tone made me wonder if this was akin to telling someone you love her ugly sweater to cover up for how much you've been staring at it.

"Thanks for having me," I said.

Celeste smiled at me—with warmth? Derision? I tried to smile back, but my lips were frozen into some kind of grimace. She was very beautiful, and it made me hate her. I wanted to excise my favorite features from her face, her body, and Jojo's, too, and I wanted to make them mine.

"Well, come in," she said, ushering us into the crowded room. "Put your coats in my room, wine's on the kitchen counter, beer in the fridge—"

"We know everything," Jojo said. "Oh! And." She reached into her handbag and pulled out a bottle of two-dollar wine.

"You *shouldn't* have." Celeste examined it. "The white, thank God. The red tastes like feet."

I looked out into the apartment. The crowd was already thick and humming. My stomach lurched, girding me for humiliation, but I saw hardly anyone else I knew. There was a long-sleeved velvet crop top over a pair of jeans with shredded knees, long brown hair chopped into bangs; a guy in a collared short-sleeved shirt with a bold jungle print; a V-neck white T-shirt. Benny was already talking to a girl in the corner, his palm flat against the wall above her shoulder. She had her head cocked and was twirling a strand of hair round and round her finger, a habit I found repulsive. Benny seemed to like it. His hand, splayed out on the wall like that, looked like a little boy's, hairless and pale. Nothing like the bartender's, those solid fingers curled around the knife. *I saw you.* He had watched me shove a dick inside my mouth, looking up at its owner like a desperate little slut, and he had seen me cry. I felt awash in fresh shame, squeezed my hands into fists to ward off the feeling. *Come back,* his note said. Why had he wanted me to come back—because he liked desperate little sluts? Because he wanted me to suck his dick, too? Because he wanted me?

Jojo wound through the throng toward Celeste's bedroom, off the living room, to store her coat, and I followed. The apartment had a French feeling, with its enormous windows, through which I could just barely make out, in the twilight, a row of pert little evergreens on the rooftop across the street. I wished I were there instead, peering in on the party from afar. Really, I wished I were back at the bar. Opposite the kitchen was a spiral staircase; Celeste rented a room out to another girl from school for cheap, and I imagined it was up there somewhere. But this was really Celeste's place. Her parents had bought it for her, I knew from Jojo; it seemed they were all too glad to lord that debt over Celeste, and she was often in turmoil about it. My parents paid half my rent—if there was one thing they had always been generous with, it was money— yet having your parents buy an apartment for you was something else. Mine surely had the money to do so, but I would never ask. The thought was ludicrous; I pictured my father giving me a dismissive smirk. But between my teaching job and the money they gave me, I made my rent. By the time I was Celeste's age, I expected I wouldn't need help at all. It was pathetic, in a way, living in an apartment your parents had bought for you, and I marveled at how she could flaunt it, how she didn't feel ashamed.

We made our way to the bedroom. I shimmied off my jacket and, in the large picture window, caught my reflection. Jojo's long legs hovered ghastly and tantalizing in the background, revealing the fraudulence of my own frame. Her back was to the window, which allowed me to stare baldly at her reflection: her green dress, with its tight bodice and short, flouncy skirt, her legs its stamen. I looked back at myself, my second-rate body in its short shirt-dress and heels. My expression looked harsh and frightening, and I smoothed out my features, offering myself a plastic smile. I held it as I blinked, like a doll.

"You look great. Let's go," Jojo said, startling me.

"One sec," I said, mortified. "I'll meet you out there."

When she'd left, I stared myself in the eyes. "I saw you," I whispered to my face, "you fucking slut." I had intended to shame myself, but this had aroused me. "I saw you, slut," I said again, looking into my eyes, and for a few moments was enveloped in a warmth that made me look beautiful to myself, before my mind reverted to its normal register and I appeared ugly again, bags under my eyes, lips pursed and thin, hair frizzing out like an electrical storm.

In the crowd, I couldn't find Jojo, so I went for the drinks table in the corner. It was already laden with used plastic cups, beads of yellow and orange and red liquid clinging to their insides. I found a sleeve of new cups under the table and poured myself a vodka with lemonade. In the center of the table, Celeste had placed a hammered silver ice bucket—parent-funded, I was sure; it looked expensive—which seemed forlorn among the tall plastic bottles of liquor and liters of soda and discarded cups. The ice had mostly melted; the silver tongs were submerged under the few remaining bits, like they had given up. I picked out a few slivers of ice with my fingers and plunked them into my cup, took a sip and let the harsh sourness burn through my chest. Everything was better with a cup of something; it gave me a place to put my hands.

I was safe in the corner. My heels were starting to dig into my anklebones. Hardly anyone else was wearing heels; skirts and dresses were almost exclusively paired with bright white sneakers and skate shoes. I had worn the heels to manufacture a sense of power and self-esteem, but now that I was here I felt absurd and wondered if I should take them off and hide them in the corner, walk around barefoot. I was trying too hard, so hard, it was obscene. But walking around barefoot—wouldn't that be even more affected?

There was a bag of ruffled potato chips open on the table, and I mechanically fed them to myself in between sips of my drink. I'd had a bowl of cereal while getting dressed for the party, but other than that, I'd hardly eaten all day. The potato chips and alcohol mixed unpleasantly with the cereal and milk, which made me eat more, as if by committing to volume, I could stuff down the displeasure.

I scanned the crowd. There was Celeste in the middle of the room, her movements growing grander. She stood with a girl and two guys, who now threw back their heads laughing at something she'd said. This made her laugh, too, her slender shoulders pitching forward, her face falling into a soft, happy reverie. Jojo had told me that her insecurities were plain, her self-doubt its own person, but at the moment that knowledge held no weight. I felt only hot jealousy.

I chewed on my thumbnail, took another sip of my drink, tried to seem nonchalant. One of the strangers glanced toward me across the room, looked me up and down, then looked away. *Ugly.* Into my mind flashed the memory of Dominic's girlfriend looking sidelong at me. I imagined him walking in, catching my eyes, noting my desperate heels and my too-short dress. *Nice dress,* his girlfriend would say, and they would laugh together. *Not leaving anything to chance tonight, are you.*

I finished my drink and poured myself another. I looked back toward Celeste, then at the people in her circle. I could see everyone's face except one of the men's. He was turned away from me, facing Celeste, and I studied the back of his head. Something about it arrested me: his hair curled at the nape of his neck, nestling into the divot there to take a little rest, like a sweet newborn animal—

So he was here.

My heart began to beat very loudly. I could tell that my mouth was open, that I was blinking too much. He tilted his head back in laughter again. Perhaps he had known I would be at this party and had come specifically to speak to me. I could go over, put on a nonchalant air, pretend we hadn't met before—*Oh, you work at which bar?*—but he was talking to *Celeste*, of all people, and didn't that just make perfect sense.

I edged closer so I could hear them.

"Oh, I *love* them," Celeste was saying. She turned toward the other man in the circle, who had stringy hair down to his shoulders. Celeste said his name, which I couldn't hear, and he jerked his head up from her body to her face. "Didn't you see them in concert?" she asked him. "Last year, in New Jersey or something?"

"Yeah, man," he said. He took a swig of his beer and then, as if he hadn't yet achieved the requisite level of chill, ran a hand through his hair. "They were fucking *incredible*. Dude's voice is sick. Just sick."

The non-Celeste woman shook her head. "Honestly, I wish we could go back to the days before music had lyrics at all," she said. "Just pure instrumental magic."

"Seriously?" the stringy-haired guy said with disdain.

"Yes!" she said, then started singing a Beethoven symphony, dancing and flinging her limbs about, clearly trying to charm the circle with her whimsy. The stringy-haired guy had his eyebrows raised, and I winced. Celeste was far more beautiful than her friend, and if she'd done the same gesture, I was sure this guy would be laughing now like a giddy baboon. I wished I could see the bartender's face—but now his head moved back and forth, a little no, cutting into the impromptu performance. She continued dancing for a moment, as if to proclaim her self-assurance, but then stopped and gave a nervous laugh.

"I can't stand instrumental music," the bartender said.

The rest of the circle waited for him to continue, and so did I. But he did not.

"Why?" the dancing woman asked, a little aggressively, maybe trying to punish him for his headshake, which she'd perhaps interpreted as condemnation or rejection. It was difficult to watch.

"It's irrational," the bartender said. "Uncontrollable." I breathed in sharply: my father, who hated my mother's classical music—one of their few incompatibilities—had said almost the exact same thing. *Primordial.* I knew the dancing woman had been singing a Beethoven symphony, I realized, because it was on one of the records my mother would play when my father wasn't home. If he came home in the middle, he'd groan, "This again!"—he'd always try to make a joke of it, but it was clear it very much wasn't a joke to him, that there was something painful about the music and he needed it to stop. Immediately, my mother would shut it off.

"Yeah, it makes you *feel*, dude," the stringy-haired man said, running his hand through his hair again, like punctuation. "That's what music is supposed to do." Never mind that he had been proselytizing someone's "sick" voice and sneering at the dancing woman only moments before. I wondered if I should insert myself into the circle to make this point in the bartender's defense, but now Celeste had taken a little step toward the bartender and was looking at him with her eyes wide and her lips pursed into a little pout—*I'm listening, I'm here for you, and also you want to fuck me.* A look that stopped me cold.

I watched as the bartender shrugged. "It's just my preference," he said in response to the stringy-haired dude, but it seemed he was looking directly at Celeste. "When my sister played the piano growing up, it bothered me so much I asked my mother to have it removed."

"Did she?" Celeste asked, and I saw that she had stepped far enough into the circle that she had almost edged out the two other people. The bartender nodded.

"Fucking *men!*" the dancing woman said, throwing her hands up.

But Celeste reached toward the bartender and laid her hand on his arm. This was more than I could stand. "You're sensitive," she said.

My stomach twisted in a queasy way. I bit my tongue to keep from doing anything stupid. *He's mine!* I wanted to yell. *Mine! She didn't even pay for this place!* Anything that would break her spell over him. Anything that would make him, instead, see me. But I did nothing. I forced myself to continue staring as the stringy-haired guy, sensing defeat, walked away, jiggling his empty cup as an excuse; I wondered if the dancing girl would do the same. Celeste had removed her hand from the bartender's arm, but there seemed to me something invisible and powerful linking them together. I took a sip of my drink—not enough—I finished it and crossed my arms and pinched the soft fold of flesh in the crook of my elbow—better—

I heard a squeal and turned to see Jojo, across the room, pushing through toward the door, where her boyfriend had just entered. He saw her and his face broke through with radiant joy. He was only half out of his jacket and let the free arm dangle as she jumped up and flung her arms around his neck; they kissed each other like they were food. It had only been a few days since they'd seen each other, by my count. What a display.

I was so caught up in watching them, it took me several moments to notice that Sam had come in behind Jojo's boyfriend. He was scanning the crowd, maybe looking for me. He wore the same blue bomber jacket he'd worn last night, hands in the pockets, creases of fabric running up toward his shoulders, which filled out the jacket with a meaty substantivity. I felt a flush of desire, as if my body were being transported back to how I'd felt when I'd first seen him or something raw were peeking out from underneath everything else. He was handsome, his sandy-blond hair falling over his forehead, his masculine features set in a disarmed, boyish expression as his eyes moved over the room. But then he saw me and smiled, too happy, and the familiar disgust washed through me. Why was he here? I hadn't replied to his texts; what kind of loser couldn't take a hint? How had he even found out about this party? Had Jojo told him? I forced a smile as he pushed his way toward me through the crowd.

"Hey again, you!" Sam said, wrapping his arms around me and drawing me to him. I gave him a taut peck, pulled back. "How come you didn't text me back?"

"My phone died," I said. "Sorry."

"It's okay, don't worry about it." I couldn't tell if he believed me. He ducked his head into my line of vision. "Hey," he said. "Is everything okay?"

"Actually, can you give me a sec? I need to talk to Jojo about something."

"Sure," he said, but furrowed his eyebrows and continued to hold me. I wriggled out from his grip.

Jojo was still pressed up against her boyfriend, her arms encircling his neck, the two of them talking closely and swaying a little, like they were dancing. I poked her on the shoulder. She looked over, startled, and I was glad to have shattered their reverie.

"I need to talk to you," I said.

"Sure, what's up?"

"In private?"

"Oh." She gave her boyfriend an apologetic smile. He kissed her on the forehead, finally taking off the other sleeve of his stupid jacket as we turned away.

I had her by the biceps, pulling her toward the nook of the kitchen, where Sam wouldn't be able to see us. I burrowed into the crowd, trying to get as deep into the corner as possible, finally arriving and facing Jojo. Her face wore a fearful expression, and I realized I was squeezing her arm so hard my nails were digging into her skin. I, too, felt startled and scared by this action, as if my hand were a being separate from me, and let the vise spring open. She held her arm to her chest, massaging it, as if to communicate to it that it was safe now, it was back in its rightful place and she would protect it from me. But then there was her expression, hard and glaring.

"What is happening?" she said.

"Did you invite Sam?"

"Yes," she said. "I did."

"Why? You knew I didn't want him here!"

"Because he's my brother? And I did want him here?" Her shoulders were pulled up toward her lovely face, she was cowering from me, but there was that fierceness there, too, so bright it made me afraid. "Besides, I thought you did want to see him, you just were playing hard to get, or maybe weren't letting yourself."

"That makes no fucking sense," I said, though my mind was swirling like a tornado. I couldn't think straight; I was scared of what my body would do next. "Sorry," I muttered, and pushed past her, jostling her.

"Wait," she called after me, "what the fuck? You're just leaving, without finishing this?"

But I walked briskly away from her, her voice melting into the loud crush of other voices. Sam was waiting for me where I'd left him, holding his jacket.

"Is everything okay?" he said again.

"Girl stuff," I said. Jojo was probably pressing toward us. I needed to get out. I could run for the bartender, grab him and pull him out of the party and onto the street— *he's mine*—but if I crossed the room to the couch, I would intercept Jojo. Besides, he probably wanted to stay with Celeste. *He's mine*, I would say, and he would shake his head, like he'd done to the foolish dancer. *No*, he would say. *Why ever would I be yours?* My heart pounded in my ears. I turned to Sam. "Want to go upstairs?"

The little curtain of the half floor had been pulled aside, and I saw that, rather than using it as a storage space, Celeste had turned it into a reading nook, filled with pillows and a tiny nightstand with a lamp. Sam and I crawled in. He closed the curtain around us and began rearranging the pillows, which had been flung about by the previous visitors, into an almond-like configuration, a little bed for us. I pushed into him, interrupting. He pressed back, ducking his head toward mine to fit beneath the ceiling. He pushed me down and rolled on top of me; I pulled him closer, until his weight oppressed me, made it hard to think. He kissed my collarbone, my neck, my jaw, my earlobe; he sucked it slowly, wending his tongue around its petal of flesh.

He paused to look at me, his hair falling around his face. It was beautiful hair, golden and soft, and I reached up to run my fingers through it. His eyes closed a little, like he was a puppy happy to be pet. I yanked his shirt over his head and he wriggled out of it; I kissed his chest, the curls of hair there reaching up toward his neck; I wrapped my legs around him and pressed into him, I bit his shoulder, he let out a moan and rolled to my side to pull my shirt up to my breasts and slip his hand beneath my underwear. He circled his finger in the slickness, I breathed into the thin skin at the base of his neck. I felt close to coming, my head light, my ears ringing a little, but then I thought of how my face would look, the gruesome contortion of it—

"You're so wet," Sam whispered, and I felt a sudden disgust at the leakage of my body in ways I had not willed, like a seeping wound. I pushed myself away from him, freeing myself from his hand, and unbuttoned his jeans. I pulled his pants down with a roughness over his cock, which sprang back to full mast. I leaned down over him, letting his dick graze my stomach, then pressed the palm of my hand to the base of it, two fingers on either side. This aroused me, the stiffness I had created with my body, and how my hand was a scissor, like I could snip it off if I wanted.

I moved myself between his legs and took him into my mouth. His head was toward the curtain and I saw that he hadn't closed it all the way, there was a sliver of space so anyone passing by could peek in. Like the bartender. And maybe this was why he had come. *Did you want to be seen?* I imagined him watching me as I sucked Sam, or, better yet, locking eyes with me while I had Sam's dick in my mouth—was this the game we were playing, me watching him with Celeste, him watching me with Sam? I straddled Sam and went to put him inside me. "Wait," he said, and reached into the pocket of his jeans, crumpled on the floor, and ripped the condom's package with his teeth and rolled it on. He gripped my sides and pushed me onto my back, the sharp suck of insertion, I wound my legs around his back, blood rushed into my pelvis, he screwed up his eyes as if there were something in me he didn't want to see, or maybe it was me who closed my eyes, I can't remember.

He was about to come. And it was just the two of us here.

"Stop," I said harshly, the command surprising both of us.

He froze. "Sorry," he mumbled. "Did I hurt you?"

"It's not that," I said, trying to modulate my voice, which only made it come out robotic. He had one hand on either side of me, his hair hanging down toward my face. I could feel him growing soft.

"Pull my hair," I commanded, and the pulsing between my legs grew more insistent.

He threaded his fingers gently through my hair and gave it a tug. His dick began to stiffen again inside me. I shook my head dismissively.

"Harder," I said.

He tugged porno-hard.

"Harder," I said. I wanted my scalp to burn. I wanted him to pull so hard he yanked out a fistful. "Harder!"

His dick had shriveled up. He released my hair and pulled out. "No," he said. "I don't want to."

"You *do* fucking want to! You *do* want to! You're just not letting yourself!"

"No," he said. "*You* want me to. You don't give a shit what I want." He had rolled off the condom and was pulling on his boxers and then his jeans and his shirt, shaking his head rapidly. "I actually like you—"

"No, you don't."

"You don't get it." He grabbed the rest of his things, opened his mouth to say something, then closed it again. He looked like a goldfish. He turned to leave the nook, moving slowly as if he hoped I would tell him to wait, but I turned my head away. Finally, he left.

I lay there on my back, shirt still pulled up past my stomach, underwear around my ankles, knees pointing into the air, until his boots stopped clanging against the spiral staircase and he was gone. I hated him! I hated Jojo for inviting him! I punched my thigh hard, then harder, until it turned white and then red, hot and inflamed. Only then could I close my eyes and breathe in, several huge, sustaining lungfuls. I touched the red spot on my leg tenderly, knowing it would leave a bruise, then pulled up my underwear, clammy and cold, and looked out of the nook. I couldn't see Sam anywhere. Jojo and her boyfriend were on the couch in the far corner. Where was the bartender? Celeste was easy to spot in her shimmery dress; she was by the drinks table, pouring herself yet another. Now she was with a bearded trust-fund painter from her year, his arm draped across her shoulders. Again I scoured the crowd. The bartender was definitely not present. My relief that he wasn't still speaking to Celeste, her hand on his arm—or kissing her in the corner, or fucking her upstairs—was enough to make me woozy. Had he gone back to Pilz Bar? My eyes landed again on Jojo, who looked upset and angry, her face splotchy, her lips pursed. She was talking to her boyfriend and shaking her head, probably telling him what a disgusting half-human I was; his arm was encircling her, he was listening and nodding, he was stroking her shoulder with her fingertips, round and round.

I scurried down the stairs, grabbed my coat and bag from the bedroom, and ran outside.

Chapter 4

When I got out, I checked my phone. Two missed calls from my mother. What I wanted was to go to Pilz Bar, but I *had* to go to my parents' first, at least for a little bit. I couldn't risk it—the fallout. It would make it more bearable, knowing I could stop by Pilz on my way home. Even if the bartender wasn't there, *someone* would be; someone always was.

I took the M86 bus across town. The Upper West Side was quiet and dark, the park a series of inkblots. I wondered if the anorexic man was still trudging through on his lonely jog. In my mind I saw his skinny muscles twitching and a hot wind of sadness blew through me. I wanted to hold his skeletal frame, rock him back and forth and say, *Shh, shh,* into his ear. It was an impulse I'd had as a teacher, seeing my students in pain: to curve myself around them, to make them mine. One student, a week prior, had come into class with splotchy eyes, and halfway through— overcome by a fresh wave of sadness about whatever was haunting her—she had spent minutes digging around in her backpack to mask her tears. All through the class, I'd tried to catch her eye, so I could mouth, *Are you okay?* Not only had I failed to do so, but I'd been so distracted by my mission, by the thick haze of her distress, that it had been difficult for me to focus on the other students. Over and over, I'd caught myself nodding in a rhythmic trance, insensate to what they were saying, and had had to snap myself back into the room. Afterward, I'd called her to my desk, and once the other students had left I'd touched her elbow and asked if she was all right. But she had only nodded and walked away, leaving me aching and hollow. That night, I had drafted and then deleted a dozen emails to her, struggling not to ask if she was okay. I had managed not to, and the next day, she was restored, it seemed. I'd felt abandoned; the feeling returned to me now, in recollecting. I looked out the bus window, then turned my focus to my reflection, there against the darkening landscape. *Hi, friend*—but I wasn't a friend, was I. Again, I imagined holding the anorexic man in my arms, soothing him—but then I pictured his face vacant and ghastly against my shoulder, his eyes unseeing, pointed toward nothing. This frightened and then incensed me, his ingratitude, and instead I pictured throwing his bony frame into the woods, his limbs splayed out in flight, his body falling to the ground with a thud. His legs like kindling, I would light them on fire.

I realized I was drunk. I let my brain swish around, the bright blue plastic of the bus seat in front of me bleeding out in hazy streaks. Who cared about Jojo? Who cared about Sam? *You don't give a shit what I want.* I took out the crumpled napkin, unfurled it. It was already fringing, but his words were still legible: *Come back. Come back. Come back.* I could go live with the bartender, never see Jojo or Sam again, or anyone I'd ever known. I felt certain he'd gone back to Pilz Bar after he'd left Celeste's—that he was holding down the space, solid and stable. Waiting and ready. I felt my body swaying of its own accord, and I liked this, as though I were dancing. My legs splayed open and this felt good, too. I was a young woman, alive and free, giving my vagina some air. There was a man in front of me, dozing with his head against the window, seeming to have just gotten off work and to be at the beginning of a long journey home. I closed my eyes and leaned my head against the window as well, but this was too swishy, the bumping of the bus along the road made me feel ill. When I opened my eyes I was nauseated and wretched again.

My mind went to my parents, whom I would only partially placate with my arrival; they would be angry I was late, they would be angry I hadn't let them know—if they weren't angry with me for what I'd done. I thought about Langham, who may or may not be there still. I didn't know what I hoped. It didn't matter, anyway, my hopes held no currency. I looked out the window as we rode through Central Park, trying to make out the trees in the darkness, to focus so hard I couldn't think anything else. But the trees were a blur.

When we exited the park, a mother stepped onto the bus, holding her baby and dragging her toddler daughter, who was wailing, by the hand. She sat the toddler down and sank next to her, looking only at the baby. The harder her toddler cried, the more her mother ignored her. She cooed at the baby, she stroked the baby's cheek, she looked out the window, away from her tortured child. For a long time I stared at the toddler, willing her to look at me, so I could offer her some company. But she only wanted her mother. Wail: *Mommy*. Wail: *Mommy*. Mommy looked away, resolute. Mommy would not help her. There was so much pain in New York you could vomit.

As I walked up Park Avenue toward my parents' building, I felt forlorn. The balls of my feet had supported my weight all night and had now had enough; the ankles had been rubbed raw underneath the protruding bones. My jacket was open, the cold air climbing up underneath my shirt, trying to wash the drunkenness away.

The awning looked sinister at this hour, casting a long sharp shadow in the streetlights. I walked toward it slowly, steeling myself, imagining what was to come. I pictured the taut-lipped look on my parents' faces. The accusations and anger—I couldn't do them the courtesy of replying? Was I ten years old? *Selfish.* Or maybe the worst would come: the punishment for Langham, whatever it might be. *How dare you.* I could deny it, but did I even want to? *You are a disgrace.* I could say I hadn't done it, that they were imagining everything—but he would be there, what would he say?—or I could take the opposite tack, own what I'd done, defend my right to sleep with whomever I wanted—or I could blame Langham; wasn't it his fault after all? how much power did I have?—but before I could think it through, before I could thoroughly prepare, the doorman had opened the door, said hello, hello, it was good to see me again, and ushered me inside.

I took the elevator up and swayed along the hallway, trailing my fingers along the wall for balance. The hallway carpet had a garish color scheme, one that had always repulsed me; tonight it felt particularly offensive, even vulgar. I wondered who would open the door, my father or my mother. Would they hug me? Would they touch me at all? Even if they didn't know about Langham, I wasn't sure. My mother would hug me and kiss me on both cheeks, but with my father, it was always an open question. Sometimes he didn't hug me at all; other times he pitched his shoulders toward mine to touch and patted my back rapidly with his palm, keeping the rest of his body at a distance. I always reciprocated, keeping my body far from his as well, creating a tent, patting his back as he pat mine. The gesture gave me an anxious, fluttery feeling, my father's distress seeping into me, and I began to feel it already as I neared the doorway.

Before I could knock, the door swung open, and there was my father, stance wide, right in the center of the doorframe. He looked like a painting, trim and handsome, hands in his pants pockets with his jacket draped behind them. I wanted to fling my arms around him and cry, *Daddy!* But his look stopped me—*calm down, calm down*—and "That's very short," he said. I froze. Maybe he hadn't meant my dress—had he meant my hair? The time it had taken my bus to cross town? No, he wouldn't know that—was it possible I had misheard? But he cut into my thoughts in a low voice: "The homeless guy on the corner doesn't need to see everything you own."

Suddenly I was too sober. Or maybe I was about to throw up. I stood incredibly still, riding the wave of panic as I pictured vomiting at my father's feet, *don't look at the carpet,* and stared at a small crack on the doorframe instead.

My eyelids fluttered like moths' wings. "I..." But I didn't know what to say. I kneaded the hem of my shirt with my fingers, pulling it as far down as I could. This only stretched the low neck farther down, and I released it, my face flushing.

Finally my father called for my mother. There were long moments of a silence so thick it held sparks. My mother arrived at the door and kissed me on both cheeks.

"You made it," she said, "we didn't know if you would."
She squeezed the back of my arm in a gesture that could
have held warmth or anger, I couldn't tell. I wondered
if she could smell the alcohol on me, if she knew I was
drunk; but they were probably at least a little drunk, too.

"I made it," I said.

My father whispered something into her ear and she
looked me up and down. I stared at her, imploring her to
chide him, to tell him I was a grown woman and could
wear what I wanted. I begged her to tell him to look at me,
I was young and beautiful and could pull off any sort of
thing. She moved toward me, put her hand on my back,
and I leaned into it, ready for her to rub her hand in circles,
to soothe me.

"Do you want to borrow something?" she whispered.

I straightened my back away from her hand like I'd
been branded. That I had leaned into it moments earlier,
looking for an ally, made clear that I was a fool. I was
ashamed, I felt exposed and whorish and was desperate
to cover myself. I would rather be wearing anything than
this dress—a sack, a trash bag. I deserved it.

The dining room table was abandoned, strewn with
chocolate-streaked dessert plates and stained wine glasses, murmurs of conversation emanating from the living
room, where the last members of the dinner party always
migrated for nightcaps. No one had seen me yet, and
this was a small mercy. I didn't know who was still here,
but I could hardly think about that right now. I needed
to change my clothes, it was urgent, imperative. In my
mother's closet, I wanted to sink underneath the dresses
and curl into a ball, hug my knees to my chest. I should

have known this outfit would make my father uncomfortable. Had I worn it particularly to provoke him? Had I purposefully left my jacket unzipped? I had meant to air myself out, I had thought, but perhaps that was only a cover for my brazen disrespect. My mother's email from this morning flashed into my mind: "You could wear the black pants." She had given me explicit instructions, she had told me exactly how to behave, and if I had obeyed her, this would not be happening. I had not listened. I had failed.

I rifled through my mother's clothing. My frame was similar to hers, but a less comely version, as if someone had made a copy of her in a great hurry and it had come out pixilated and lumpen. Her clothes fit me poorly, the *almost* of them highlighting just how much better they looked on her. I chose a pair of black slacks that hung off her hips like a waterfall. On me they gaped in awkward places, looked like dress-up, nothing like real glamour. I tucked my shirt in. I wanted to leave. I wanted to climb out my parents' bedroom window. I wanted to go back to Pilz Bar. I wanted the bartender to watch over me while I napped, so I could sleep in peace knowing I was safe. Could I go back to the bar and ask to just sleep for a bit, ask him to sit in a chair while I closed my eyes? Would he ask me what I'd been up to since we'd met, where I had been? I wondered what he'd say about Sam, about him pulling my hair, about *harder! Harder!* I wondered what he'd say about Langham. The thought of telling him made me nauseated, my throat tightening around the feeling— but there was relief there, too, that someone might know. Maybe he knew already. Those eyes. Maybe he possessed a mystical omniscience, knew where I was and what I'd been doing this whole evening long. Maybe he was with me now, in this closet, his hand on the small of my back.

I edged into the doorway of the living room, trying to observe the group in secret, to take stock before I plunged in. The room was always the same, the curtains of the wide window pulled open onto the landscape of the city at night, the decorative pillows on the couch so numerous you had to stack them to sit down, on the wall the framed series of paintings my parents had bought on the street during their honeymoon in France. On the table that abutted the couch was the award my parents had won a few years before, from the Association for Behavioral and Cognitive Therapies, for a paper they'd published together. This was unusual, but not exactly rare. They had different subspecialties, but since they co-owned the practice, from time to time they collaborated on research. I hated it.

My father was holding court, talking about one of his clients, gesturing with a cut crystal glass. Every few lines of speech, he would raise the glass to his lips and take a small sip, but he made sure to begin the next sentence first to ensure that he would continue to be granted the floor. "So"—sip—"after a few weeks of thought tracking, she seemed to have improved..." As always, I wondered about his client, what he was like in her company, whether he was as directive with her as he could be with me. I knew there was a tenderness deep inside him—I'd seen it myself, in that first moment when he would touch the back of my neck so gently. Or that time, as a child, I'd been playing with his reading glasses. I had found them on the kitchen table while my parents were still at work next door and had put them on, checked myself out in the mirror. Inspired by my reflection—the glasses were rectangular, making me look smart and almost adult, even as they slid down my nose—I'd edged into his closet to explore his clothes. This wasn't a strictly forbidden zone, but on any given day invading his privacy in this way might infuriate him. That day, though, since I didn't expect them back home for a while, I'd put on one of his suit jackets, the arms dangling down around my hands. I'd sat in the armchair across from their full-length mirror and was furrowing my eyebrows at my reflection, nodding at myself, just like I imagined he must have been doing across from a patient in his office at that very moment, when he walked in. I froze, the hairs along my neck and arms standing at attention—but for some reason he started to laugh. "That's funny," he'd said, shaking his head. "Boy, that's funny."

It was this version of him that I imagined he let flourish in the office. The one who laughed. The soft one. I had ruined my chance, hadn't I, with my fucking outfit! How could I have been so stupid? I had been too much myself. I wanted to go back—to put on his jacket again, his glasses, anything to get him to look at me that way. Like he looked at his clients, probably. I felt a flush of rage, thinking of them, the recipients of his careful attentions. Why them? Why not me? But I knew why—it was because I did things like this: Like exposing my body in such a repulsive way. Like fucking Langham. Their colleague! And there he was, kitty-corner from my father, nodding along to his speech. Everyone was, their supplicant expressions reminding me of Celeste in her coterie of admirers, even my mother, who deferred to him with almost the same quality of admiration as their colleagues. Of course they were; he was *him*. I watched Langham squint in performative concentration. I felt ill. Why had I come? Could I still leave? But if they didn't know—or even if they did—wouldn't my abrupt departure, without even speaking to their guests, be its own grave sin? I had to stay at least an hour. I could do that much, couldn't I? I edged into the doorway. Langham didn't look up, but I saw his posture stiffen, and I knew he knew I was there.

I walked in, the ill-fitting slacks crinkling with each step. "There she is," my father said, cutting into my thoughts, and I was so relieved to be his prize again I almost giggled, the kind of laugh that made people uncomfortable. Instead I managed to only smile at my father; he winked at me, and the intimacy of this gesture was nearly too much to stand. My mother ushered me in, her hand on my back once more, and I made the rounds of hugs, trying my best to ignore Langham. Would my parents be acting this way if they knew? It was entirely possible; this would not be the moment they'd choose to punish me. Appearances were paramount. Whatever it was would come later. *Hi, so good to see you*. I breathed in their colleague Patrice's familiar floral perfume and her husband's musky scent, which reminded me pleasantly of a horse stable. They were good together, had always been, not in the powerful, star-crossed, showy way of my parents, but in a lower key. Their son, Leroy, who was a few years younger than me, hadn't come for years now: he'd recently started college, but even in high school, he'd had other plans, and whenever his parents had rotated in among the guests, they'd let him skip. The one time I'd mentioned that I wanted to go to a friend's place instead, that I wouldn't be able to make it, my mother had breathed an *oh* with such wounded shock that I'd retracted immediately. She was too fragile; it would break her. Or she was too proud, unable to countenance that I'd want anything other than the life they'd built, even for a moment. I didn't know. It didn't matter; I'd never tried again—not until the four-year respite of college. But now I was back, and back meant here, in their apartment. Why did Leroy get to be free?

My aunt and uncle had left, it seemed. The only remaining guest was a woman a bit older than me, and my mother introduced her as their young new colleague Olivia. Her black hair was cut into a blunt bob, one side tucked behind her ear, the other covering a bit of her face in a becoming way. She was pretty. Langham was to my left, and I made a show of introducing myself to Olivia, smiling beautifully and magnanimously. Langham who? But my mother touched my arm and gestured to the left.

"You're forgetting Dr. Langham," she said, steering me toward him.

So they didn't know.

My body went heavy, my throat tight; it took everything I had not to cry. But why? Wasn't this a good thing? They hadn't brought me here to punish me! They just wanted me here, their daughter! Tears pricked at the backs of my eyelids.

They didn't know.

But Langham did. Langham, my coconspirator. My secret accomplice. We had done something wrong, and we had gotten away with it. "I'm sorry," I said to him. "It's nice to see you again." I tried to look up at him from under my eyelashes in a way he would find attractive—*this is our secret*—I needed the laser beam that had connected us last week—*they don't know*—but he returned my gaze with a neutral expression, then pursed his lips, not only failing to be aroused by me, but actively putting me off. His lips said, *This is not going to happen*. His lips said, *I don't want you*.

"Nice to see you," he said. He pumped my hand. A sour taste flooded my mouth and I swallowed and backed away. All at once I could hardly stand wearing my mother's slacks for one more second, these beautiful pants that looked absurd on me, like a satin ribbon tied around steaming summer trash. I had thought that Langham and I had a secret, but I was alone! I'd thought I was better than him, that I'd done him a favor, but it turned out that he was better than me! He had rejected me! It was astonishing—it was right—he had taken a taste and decided he could acquire someone of more worth. Well, he could. I was nothing.

Meanwhile my father had taken it upon himself to extol my successes to the assembled guests. Did they know that I had been granted a competitive fellowship as a first-year English teacher at the exclusive prep school blocks away? No matter that my mother, who was friendly with the dean of the school, was more than likely the reason I had gotten the post, nor that I had been a student there myself, and that my parents had paid full tuition. These elements did not pertain to the narrative my father was now performing, and he did not mention them. I exhibited what I hoped resembled a smile as my mother picked up the narrative, telling the guests that my college thesis had received a prize. I knew I should appreciate these gestures of pride on my parents' part, but they felt bizarrely unrelated to me, to the rotten core of me, curdled and festering.

Moments later, with an "Anyway—," my father picked back up on the conversation I had interrupted, continuing to detail the intricacies of his apparently quite successful case. I lowered myself onto the arm of the couch and tried to follow the conversation, to distract myself, but my ears rang and I couldn't make out the words. I looked out the window: a quilt of tiny lights. It was the last thing my mother always did when preparing for guests: plump the pillows, smooth the coverlet of the couch, then pull the curtains way to the side. *Our city.* I always marveled at the baldness of this claim of ownership, how gauche it was. And yet I also swooned at the view, at the Chrysler Building in particular, its arches of light reaching up into the black sky. It had always been my friend, and I telegraphed a silent plea to it now, as I had so many times before. *Save me, watch me, hold me.* It *was* beautiful, the view my parents had purchased, the image of man's creation they now owned. Perhaps I was envious. Or perhaps I was repulsed by my attraction to it, which meant I was as materialistic as they.

My mother tipped her glass of wine toward me across the room with a questioning look. I nodded. As she poured me a glass, she mouthed, *Dinner?* But at this I shook my head. She had betrayed me, earlier, in the doorway, and I would not let her feed me now. *Cake?* I dislodged myself from the exchange and examined Olivia, her pert bob, her sweet black dress with three-quarter-length sleeves and a wide boatneck that reached almost to her shoulders. There was something familiar about the cant of her shoulders, and I thought of Client Z, the young bulimic my father had treated when I was a child. I examined Olivia's face. It had been so long I could hardly recall—though yes, I felt certain it was she. She was no longer noticeably thin with a puffy face; her body and face matched now, her hair looked healthy and clean. Why had he even treated her, when eating disorders were my mother's specialty? I remembered seeing Client Z through the peephole near the end of her treatment, laughing at something my father had said before she entered the office and closed the door. I had felt betrayed and frantic, beholding her, and these sensations flooded me once more. How had she transitioned from patient to colleague? How did he feel about her now? My heartbeat kicked up into my throat—Sam entered my mind, then Jojo—their certain hatred of me— these thoughts were painful, but the pain was comfortable, it was better, it was my home.

My mother rose out of her seat to hand me the glass of wine, and I took big sips of it, looking toward Patrice. She was gesturing toward my father, offering feedback on his case. Her gestures were large, overly so, and I got the sense that she was desperate to hold my father's attention, to provide feedback that he approved of and was impressed by. He was looking at her, but without the studied interest I could tell she was seeking. She wore a shapeless dress— purple, the most classless color—and something about it made me feel intensely sorry for her. I had the urge to hug her, to ferret her away from here. My father sat still as a statue, bizarrely not giving so much as a nod of gratitude for her insights, which to my mind were sharp. *Asshole*.

The napkin was with my jacket, hanging in some closet of this apartment. What was the bartender doing right this minute? Was he still on his shift? By now the bar crowd would be thick, the room steamy. I craved that feeling; it gave me a sense of safety, like the crush of a subway during rush hour, my chest pressed up against some man's distended stomach, or my nose inches from a woman's floral-shampooed hair, or my head so close to a hairy arm, outstretched toward the pole, that I could almost use it as a pillow. I pictured the bartender's face, imagined pressing my thumbs along those eyebrows, his eyes floating closed; I would bite his bottom lip, a surprise.

I glanced at Langham again. He looked resolutely away from me. His eyes followed the conversation like a schoolchild's. When the line of conversation required his gaze to pass over me, he managed to avert it, either blinking briefly or flitting his eyes down underneath me and back up again. He had no problem looking at Olivia. Would he try to fuck her, too? Olivia. Client Z. But she wouldn't do it, would she? She was too valuable for such things. She was beautiful. She had on a fucking velvet dress. And, of course, she was *cured*. I clasped my hands together and remembered Langham's businesslike handshake moments earlier, then that very hand awkwardly caressing my face just one week ago while I lay on my father's closet floor. Again the image of his hairy belly pushing between my legs flashed into my mind and I looked down at his real belly, now in front of me once more, his pin-striped button-down straining around it. *Remember how you laughed when I licked right underneath your mustache?* I wanted to say. *Remember how it made your gut jiggle?* I wanted to screw up my face into the grimace he wore when he came. *Remember this?* But he wouldn't even look at me. He thought I was vile.

The tip of my tongue found its way again to the roof of my mouth, probing the ridge that ran down the middle. One side of it had what felt like a seam, while the other melted away. My tongue pressed back and forth along the ridge, over the hump near my throat into the softness behind, back down toward my teeth, where it found those ripples. Tap the teeth, back over the ripples, one, two, three, four, five, six... I lost count as they, too, melted away and ran my tongue back along the ridge again, digging it into the seam, noticing for the first time that it felt just like the vein threading its way along the underside of every dick. I released my tongue from the roof of my mouth, tried to hold it in space, not let it touch a thing. Nothing was a home, nothing was safe, not even the inside of my own mouth.

The familiar desperation began to bubble inside of me. I could hardly sit still, my skin was prickling and tingling. I wanted to rip it off in a clean sheath. I looked around the room, from my mother to my father to Patrice, all focused on one another, obsessed, entranced. My mind seemed to exist on a separate plane. Perhaps I was an alien, sent to observe these bobbleheads and report back to my home planet. But this game, this fantasy, did nothing to help contain me. My emotions were hot and lurid, so immense

I was floored no one else could feel them. It seemed to me I was bleeding out, my anguish flooding into the room. I wanted to squeeze my eyes shut and push out a high-pitched noise, all the muscles tightening in my stomach, my throat straining and aching with the effort, anything to dispel these dark energies. I had the urge to reach down into my underwear and almost did so, then remembered with a start that I couldn't do that here. I clanked my empty wineglass onto the floor and lurched upward.

"I have to use the bathroom," I blurted out.

On the way there, I passed the bookcase at which Langham and I had first kissed. Could it have been only one week ago? The spines of the books swam before me. I felt unsteady and gripped the side of the bookcase for support. There was the book we had laughed over: *How could anyone possibly read six hundred eighty-three pages on the history of the* zipper? He had looked at me, I knew, with craving. But it all felt unreal to me now, our shared laughter, the arousal, the pleasure of knowing with certainty I was desired. I could not even conjure his old expression, only the face he'd worn moments ago, resolutely detached, skimming over me as if I no longer existed. I imagined asking him what had happened, how it had gone wrong, and his voice echoed through my mind: *Did you really think I'd be interested in someone like you?* Maybe he had fucked me as a way to conquer my parents. *I was drunk,* he might say. Why had he called me this past week? Was it to ask if I would be here tonight, so he would know not to come? Was it to ask me, explicitly, not to? *You look nothing like I remembered. I got it all wrong. Someone's thirsty...* I wanted to run to the bartender, throw myself onto him, press myself into him, my face into his chest.

My phone buzzed. Langham had texted from the other room:

Thx for pretending nothing happened.

I wanted to ravage, I wanted to cry, I wanted to be ravaged, I wanted to be held. I wanted to be fucked, was what I really wanted. To lie still and dead and be ransacked. I wanted to be thrown around like a doll, limp and ragged, and ripped apart.

The phone buzzed again:

Heading home, take care.

And then I noticed, farther up on the home screen, that I had missed several texts from Jojo in the past couple of hours.

Did you seriously just leave this party without telling me?

Where are you?

Are you with Sam? I can't find him.

Where the fuck are you?

I ran to my old bedroom and closed the door and threw myself onto the bed. The room was still covered in the daisy-patterned wallpaper that had adorned it all my childhood. An image came into my mind—ripping my limbs from my body and roasting them over a pit; popping my head off and throwing it against the wall to explode like a pumpkin—and I squeezed my eyes shut against it, rubbed myself with an angry fervor. My heartbeat quickened, my breath quickened, the backs of my legs were sweating. New images burst forth: thick hands on my thighs; a stingray; a laugh; being flipped roughly over; patio guy's big bumpy knee; a hand on my neck; the twin knobs of his collarbone; the spire of a building; the swish of a cape; a man's ass; a swoop of hair; the bartender. I tilted my pelvis up toward my right hand, grabbed my ass with my left, my fingernails digging into my flesh. His cheekbones casting shadows, his beard, his eyes. *I saw you.* The movement of his forearm over the bar, the circles of his hand as he wiped it down, the other hand balanced against the bar. His eyes, boring into me. His hand in my hair, twisting my head around to meet his gaze. *Freud would understand.* The daisy-patterned wallpaper. The latticework of my radiator. *I saw you.* His beard, his eyes, his forearms with the muscles moving underneath, the radiator and its interlocking shapes, his sturdy fingers, the hair at the nape of his neck, our bodies pressed together. *Come back.* The carved-out shapes of the radiator, the small spaces between our bodies, *Did you want to be seen?* He was the one person who knew me, he was not a contemptuous judge, he was protector, he was possession, he was mine, I was his.

He was Freud. Sigmund Freud, bartender.

I knew he was Freud the way you know, in a dream, that a woman is your mother, even if she looks like no one you've ever seen before. When I came, I buried my mouth in my shoulder to stop myself from screaming.

Afterward, I lay on my bed, so giddy I felt like laughing. I looked to the shelf above my childhood desk, where stuffed animals still sat three rows deep—my parents had talked about turning my bedroom into a guest room, but as yet, they hadn't.

"It's funny, isn't it," I whispered to the plush teddy bear who had guarded my sleep so many nights. I didn't know if I meant my orgasm, which often made me laugh with relief, or my realization that I had met, that I now knew, that I now *had*—Freud.

I went to the door and pressed my ear against it, trying to make out the voices. There were my father's tones, the woodsy depth of them. And then a bouquet of laughter, my mother's bursting loudly above the rest. I couldn't make out Langham's, but I guessed it wasn't there.

I plucked my underwear from the floor and pulled it back on, then the slacks—and then, in a wave of pique, ripped them off again. I wasn't gross! Freud had said so! What did I need to hide myself for? I folded the pants and, on my way back out, laid them on the corner of my parents' bed. Their bedroom was as tasteful as the rest of the apartment—plush neutrals—and as scrubbed clean of personality. My mother got great pleasure out of the compliments she received from guests, even on her bedroom. They presented well, my parents. And so had I.

As I passed the bookcase once more, I searched for Freud's book, something I had not done in a very long time. When I found it, I spent a few minutes just stroking the spine, wondering if I should dare. Finally I couldn't stand it anymore and slid it out to hold.

There he was. I felt weak with relief. I traced his face with my finger, his body, his hand. I pressed my mouth to the cover, so softly, and when I lifted it away there was the faintest spot of wet. My mark. I slid it back onto the shelf.

Patrice and her husband were the only ones still in the living room with my parents. Langham had left, and

Olivia, too—so they *were* fucking. I should have yelled out, *Bulimic!* as soon as I'd realized who she was; Langham would have known, then, that she was as disgusting as I. My parents and the Lyles were hunched toward each other, whispering, as I approached. About what?—me? I strained to hear what they were saying, watched Patrice tuck her hair behind her ear, my mother shift closer to my father. I couldn't hear a word. The floorboards sang out under me and my mother glanced up. My father followed, flicked his eyes down to my bare legs, then back up to my face. I looked away. At once, the old feelings returned, the sense that I was falling. My anxiety sprang up, trying to help me grab on to something, but I was like a cartoon cat grasping at flimsy tree branches as he tumbled into a chasm. But— Freud. I had a secret. My parents hated Freud as much as they hated me—but now we had each other.

"Come in," said my mother.

"Actually..." I said. I cleared my throat, preparing myself: *Actually, I'm leaving. Actually, I'm tired, I'm going to go. I think I'm going to call it a night.* I had made it an hour, and that was what I had promised myself. I had done it, and now I could go. "Where did you put my jacket?" I blurted out, too abruptly.

"You're leaving?" she said. "Already? You've hardly been here."

The familiar tension overtook me—the desperation to leave, stopped by the knowledge that I could not. The anxiety that rose in me at these moments was almost unbearable, clouding my vision. I wanted to throw myself on my mother, to beg her to give me her blessing to leave, her promise she would still love me.

But now I had Freud. I saw in my mind his face, looking out over the bar, those thick eyebrows, the thin mouth, exactly as they were on the cover of the book and then in my memory all these years. His strong hand, gripping the knife, slicing lemons. *I saw you,* he'd said, and *Who said it was gross?* and *Did you want to be seen?* His face, beaming out toward me in my childhood fantasies, *bad girl,* looking into my eyes. *Freud would understand.* He was my teammate, my partner, my protector, my savior, my hero, my guardian, my God. Freud loved me. Freud would never leave me. *Studies, data, efficacy,* my parents had said. *Sem-i-nal!* my mother had sung. But now Freud was here, he had come for me, we were one.

"Yes," I said slowly. "I have to go. Can you tell me where my jacket is?" My jacket; the napkin.

"I understand," my mother said, pronouncing the statement with finality. It meant: *You are hurting me.* I stood inert. She got up and brushed her palms along her pants, smoothing them, then retrieved my jacket from the closet by the front door and handed it to me. My father did not rise.

"You'll come for dinner next weekend, won't you?" she said.

Next weekend. The cycle would begin again: the indecision, the dread, the guilt, the despair.

But that was for later. Now was for Freud. I slipped my hand into my pocket. *Come back.*

"I'll let you know," I said.

My mother nodded, her expression disappointed but resolute, as if she could expect no better from me than ingratitude and pain. My throat tightened.

"I'm sorry," I whispered.

She put her hand on my arm. "Get home safe," she said, and leaned in to hug me, her shoulders delicate in my embrace.

"I love you," I said, squeezing her tightly, wanting to melt into her, but when she pulled away her lips were taut. *Mommy.* "Are you mad at me?"

"No," she said, in a tone that meant she was very angry indeed, "we just miss you." I glanced at my father, but he was looking down, away from me.

And I left.

Chapter 5

When I arrived at Pilz Bar, he was standing outside, smoking, looking off down the street. The smoke drifted toward me through the night and I felt it on the back of my tongue. He looked beautiful, transforming the garbage-strewn street, shapes lurking in the streetlamped murk, into something sublime. I wanted to consume him. I wanted him to consume me.

On the long subway ride back to Brooklyn, after I'd left my parents', one phrase had echoed through my mind: *You are Freud.* I pictured saying it to him, over and over: *You are Freud, you are Freud, you are Freud.* I saw his eyes dilate, the pupils so big they could swallow me whole. *Yes,* I heard him say, *yes.* The world rose up shimmering to meet his yes. His yes was lying on my back in the park looking up at autumn leaves, his yes was a Manhattan avenue sparkling late into the night, his yes was the crescendo of an orchestral movement, his yes was being crushed, his yes was relief, his yes was warmth, his yes was home. I imagined running my hands along his sides, up and down; looking into each other's eyes. Just that. He had come back for me. I was not no one. I was not alone. *You are Freud. Yes, I am Freud. Yes.*

And here he was. His beard like brush, waiting for a fire. His arms, which had lurked in the back of my mind all night, the muscles moving beneath the skin. His sturdy frame, which could immobilize me. How many flavors of craving there are. He finished his cigarette and stubbed it out, and when he looked up, he saw me. His eyes.

"You came back," he said.

"I came back."

We stared at each other. He put his hands in his pockets. He was smiling, a little, and this made my heart race.

You are Freud.

Say it: *You are Freud.*

Instead my feet walked toward him of their own accord. I breathed him in, the pungent smell of male sweat. I raised my eyes to his and held his gaze, a look I'd given hundreds of times before, a look that meant *kiss me*, a look that meant *I'm yours*, a look that meant *yes*.

Almost imperceptibly, he shook his head.

Shame engulfed me; I was reeking of it, as if I'd soiled myself. I felt enormous and floating, obtrusive, unhidable.

I wanted to die. I wanted to disappear.

I wanted anyone else. I wanted Sam, I wanted Dominic, I wanted patio guy, I wanted Langham. I wanted to be flattened. I wanted to be small. I wanted my parents, I wanted to curl up in my mother's closet alone. Only they understood me. Freud did not understand me. Only my parents understood me—where were my mother's pants, where was her smell, where was my father's wink, I should never have left, I needed to go home.

And why had I come, when I had seen what I had at the party? Was I really and truly out of my mind?

"You want Celeste," I said, by which I meant that I was a fool, I knew I was nothing, nothing. Of course he wouldn't want me, no one would. Especially Freud. Freud, who I'd been convinced since I first saw his face staring out at me from the cover of the book—cigar in one hand, eyes burning—was my watcher, my protector, my savior. The only one who understood me, my confidant, my home. I ran my tongue along the ridge of the roof of my mouth and then remembered, with disgust, that it was just another dick. I had no home.

"You want fucking *Celeste*," I said again, to make him admit it. But he only stood there, looking at me.

"Why do you need me to betray you?" he said finally.

"*Need* you to?" I said, and, unaccountably, began to laugh—not a normal laugh, full of warmth and invitation, but a careening screech of a laugh, a car flying through the guardrail. "Need you to, when you're the one who wants Celeste instead of me, who tells me to come back and then shakes his head when I try to—when I just—when all I want—"

"What *is* it you want?" he said, cutting into my hysterics, which abruptly stopped. I wanted to fuck him, didn't I? I wanted him to hold me. "What is it you *really* want?"

But I couldn't say it. He was taunting me, trying to make me beg him, only to reject me once more. Was he seeing how much power he could wield? Was he trying to see how foolish I could be? He had orchestrated my shame; he had willed my humiliation.

"Why do you need me to betray you?" he repeated, and before I knew what my hands were doing I was trying to shove him backward into the wall. It was the first time I had touched him, and his chest was harder than I had imagined. I felt a twist between my legs. I registered what I was doing—I was touching Sigmund Freud, I was invading his space, I was assaulting him, I was caressing him—

and, as if to make sense of my action, shoved him harder. He hardly budged; he grabbed my wrist.

"Stop pushing me, please," he said.

"Let go of me," I said, but *Don't let go,* I thought.

He released me. "Why did you do that?" he asked.

"Because—" I sputtered, desperate to prove I was angry at him, not that I simply wanted, *needed,* to touch him. "Because you made me come back here, because you rejected me, because you humiliated me, because—"

"Humiliated," he said. "Betrayed. I wonder what purpose this narrative serves."

"It serves the purpose of making me feel like shit!" I screamed. But at the same time there was a glimmer of understanding: this was not what he'd meant.

"Who do you really feel rejected by?"

"You," I said.

"Is it really me?"

Who did I feel rejected by? My vision clouded, the question was too much, it made my ears ring, *She's being a baby*—who had said this?—a bright whiteness overtook my mind, a sound like static, blotting out the words—

"Sorry," I said, "I'm sorry, I should go—"

"What for?"

"For screaming at you, for being so angry, it's ridiculous, I don't even know why—"

"What's wrong with anger?"

"You said 'stop'!" I yelled. "Didn't you? You said that!"

"I said to stop pushing me, not to stop being angry," he said. "What is wrong with anger?"

"Being calm is better, anger makes you look bad, it's unseemly—"

"Where are these words coming from? Whose words are they?"

"They're mine," I said. "I'm talking. Me."

"Are they yours?"

"I don't know," I said.

Who else's words could they be? I had said them with my own mouth. But that phrase was worming its way back into my mind, *She's being a baby,* and I realized it was echoing through my memory in a man's voice. Whose? I played the tape again and an image resolved into focus: the inside of a taxicab, black leather, the filmy window separating me from the driver. I was a child—I knew this because I was wearing soft, thick black tights, a pair that my mother had thrown out not long after, to be replaced with sheer stockings. My parents were outside the taxi, trying to get me to come out; I had been in a rage, I couldn't remember what about, but my cheeks were slick with tears. I remembered willing myself to stop crying, but I could not; I remembered my father yanking my arm, trying to pull me out of the car, but I refused to budge, just continued to cry and cry. "She's being a *baby*," he had said to my mother, voice icy and hollow, and I had looked out the cab door and seen his face, like he wished I had never been born. I didn't remember what my mother had said in return, just her pursed lips. But it was my father's face that had stayed with me, a face I had seen other times when I had been too much to handle, times when I had revealed the depths of who I really was.

"What are you thinking?" said Freud, and I told him my memory.

"It sounds like his response was quite painful for you," Freud said, and I felt the urge to cry.

"But he was right!" I said. "I'm sure they were bringing me someplace wonderful, and I had to ruin it!"

He stood there silently, just looking at me. A man walked by in shorts, and I watched the thick muscles of his thighs jiggle and then clench with each step, both supple and firm, like Jell-O. Muscles, hair, skin. He had a tattoo on the back of one calf; I could just make it out as he walked away into the darkness, a geometric shape comprising thin black lines. I wanted to run my fingers along it, so lightly it would make his hairs stand on end. I looked back at Freud.

"Why don't you want to fuck me?" I whimpered.

"Why do you think you are so fixated on that question?"

I wanted him to say it: That I was disgusting. That I was ugly, repulsive, too much, and that he did not want me. I wanted the finality of it, the closure: I wouldn't have to wonder any longer, could put an end to this craving— this excruciating craving! Or was there more—that he *couldn't* want me? That for him to fuck me, he'd have to be real?

"I just want to know," I said. "I want you to say it."

"Say what?"

"That I'm disgusting." This was all I could bear. "Say it: I'm disgusting, and you don't want me. Say it! Please!" Or: *Tell me you are Freud. Tell me you've come back for me. Tell me I'm special, tell me we're a team, tell me we are one.*

"No."

"Why not? Why?" This was it, this was the moment, this was the end.

"Because that's not how I feel."

"Yes, it *is*. It is how you feel!"

"No. It's how *you* feel."

"Is not."

"You're desperate for someone to see you, but it's been so long you don't know anymore how to let yourself be seen."

I was so pained by his words it was all I could do not to smack him. "That's a whole lot of bullshit to spin."

"Maybe," he said. "Is it?"

"Fuck me," I said. "Please. Please!"

"If you sleep with me, you'll have to dispose of me. Do you really want to dispose of me?"

His question made me dizzy. I imagined pouring all the men I'd ever fucked down the drain of a sink, then flipping a switch to shred them all to pieces. The grating hum of them being ground to a pulp, then sucked away. My head spun. I leaned against the wall beside him. I don't know how much time passed without anyone saying a word. Night presented itself more fully. The smell of burning leaves emanated from somewhere, my favorite scent of fall. It made me think of a family, far away, in some wooded place, in some long-buried year, sitting in front of a fireplace, someone in a rocking chair, someone in a bathrobe, books, crackling, calm, snow outside, but inside, safe. My eyelids began to droop, my limbs grew heavy as clay—abruptly I had entered the state of drunkenness where continuing to keep my eyes open felt heroic.

"I'm going to go," I said.

He paused for a long moment, as if giving me room to change my mind. When I didn't speak, he said, "Come back."

"And why should I come back?"

"Aren't you curious?"

I walked home, zigzagging along the sidewalks. I don't remember most of the walk; the screen flickers. I knew Freud, I was certain I knew him, just as I'd known every man I'd ever fucked, every man I'd ever seen. As I neared my street, the sky was filling with pink. There it was, finally in view: my apartment, my bed—heaven. All I had to do was take about twenty more steps, find my keys, unlock the door, haul myself up the stairs, brush my teeth, undress, and then I could sleep, sleep, sleep.

But—Jojo. Not my apartment: *our* apartment. Would she be home? My nails in her skin. *I thought you did want to see him...or maybe weren't letting yourself.* She would excoriate me for yelling at her, for hurting her, for leaving the party, and, above all, for whatever she'd found out about Sam. Would he have told her? Part of me thought it unlikely: Who would tell his sister about fucking her roommate, how right in the middle she'd stopped him, commanded he pull her hair, how he hadn't been able to do it, how he'd been so scared his dick had gone soft? But part of me knew he wouldn't have to say all that. He could just as easily say I was crazy, a crazy bitch, and wouldn't Jojo agree? She could be sleeping now, it was so late, or she could be at her boyfriend's. I prayed she would be. But she could also be home, she could be awake, she could lay into me, kick me out of the apartment even. Where would I go? Where would I live? As long as I could avoid her, I could keep my home. I couldn't go back to Freud;

he had locked the door of the bar as I left. I could sleep on the street. I could get hit by a car. But twenty steps had passed. I had arrived. I would be as silent as I could, see if I could avoid her. I walked up the stairs that stretched over our landlady's garden apartment to our door. *How the fuck could you do that to Sam?* I found my keys. *How could you treat him that way—my brother?* My hands shook. But it was possible she wasn't there, she could be at her boyfriend's, or still at the party, or maybe she was with Sam right now, hearing the whole story—*unbelievable, she is unbelievable*—plotting their revenge. I unlocked the door. My ears rang. She would kick me out of the apartment, she would tell everyone she knew.

I pushed open the door to our apartment. Jojo was sitting on the stairs that led up to the second floor, to my room. I stood frozen in the doorway.

"You can come inside," she said. Her face was in the shadows and I couldn't make out her expression. I edged into the apartment and closed the door behind me, but didn't lock it, in case I needed to bolt.

"Have you been sitting here waiting for me?" I said.

"I was just talking to Sam." She had her phone in one hand and tapped it against her other palm a few times, like a baseball bat.

"I'm really sorry," I said. I felt faint and wondered if I would pass out.

"For which parts?"

"All the parts."

"List them."

I couldn't bring myself to describe my behavior, it felt like a step too far. If I started speaking, would I ever stop?

Would I tell her I'd put my fingers around Sam's dick like scissors? Would I tell her how much I'd wanted him to hurt me? Would I keep going, tell her about my parents, how my mother was ashamed of me, how my father was disgusted by me? Worst of all, would I tell her about Freud? I couldn't say anything, if I said one thing I would say everything, and if I said everything I would have nothing left.

"What did Sam tell you?" I asked.

"Not much," she said. She remained sitting, elbows propped on her knees, holding her phone between them, but her posture straightened as I approached. Her hair, in a ponytail, was curled around the side of her neck to rest on her collarbone. "He told me he made it clear he liked you," she said, eyeing me, but I didn't respond. "And that something happened. He didn't tell me what, but after what happened between *us*"—here she stretched out her arm, the one I had grabbed—"I can imagine."

"What did he say, exactly?" I edged toward her. So I'd touched her arm—so what? So I'd wanted Sam to hurt me—did that make me a villain? "Did he say I was a crazy bitch? I wanted him to pull my hair. Okay? That's it. Do we live in the fucking nineteenth century?" My voice had gone cold, my eyes narrow. I felt vicious.

"It sounded like maybe it wasn't what you did, but the way you did it," she said, matching my tone, even adding a layer of pretentious lilting, like she was explaining a simple concept to a simple child. Her jaw was clenched, but I could see her knuckles white around her phone: Anger? Fear?

"Why did you introduce me to him, anyway?" I said. "You knew what I was! Why did you even let me live here?"

"What?" she said, squinting, as though she were genuinely puzzled.

"We went to the same school."

"I didn't know that much about you, to be honest," she said.

"You knew I was a slut!"

She shook her head, bewildered.

"Don't joke," I said. "Don't lie. I know people talk."

"Not really," she said. "Anyway, there's nothing wrong with sleeping around. Who would I be to judge that?"

"But you are judging!" I said, and saw her shake her head, her expression softened and sad. She had reversed course too suddenly, and I realized why: though I wasn't crying—I was trying desperately not to—I could feel the heat in my face. I tried to summon back my anger. "Why would you introduce me to Sam if you knew?" I said. "Why? And why would you even let me live here?"

"Okay, first of all, I didn't introduce you to Sam, we all just happened to be out together last night," she said, and my face flushed with hurt again, she was right—"but, *but*, when I saw he liked you, I was happy for him, for both of you. I mean, why not? Same reason I gave you the room—I mean, I needed to fill it quickly—but! *But!* I really liked you, remember, you brought over the chocolates"—my mother's suggestion—"we talked for an hour about Tolstoy, you asked all about my thesis—"

"I made a good first impression," I said.

"That's not what I'm saying. And I don't care who you sleep with, I don't care what you do, *except* when it's with my brother," she said. "I love him, my siblings are the most important people to me in the world, and he feels like shit right now."

Love me like you love Sam, I thought. *Love me.*

"I'm sorry," I said again, "for all the parts, like I said."

"It's okay," she said.

"For being an asshole, a despicable person," I said, and she began to shake her head, "for treating your brother like shit, I obviously don't deserve him or anyone, for grabbing your arm, it was a horrible thing to do—"

"It's okay," she said, and I knew I had warped the conversation so that now she was comforting me, but I couldn't help myself. "It's okay, you can stop, I forgive you." She had realized I was a pathetic creature, not the formidable one she thought she'd been addressing.

"I can move out," I said.

"What?"

"Isn't that what you were about to say? You've realized what I'm really like, who I really am, and you want me to move out?"

"No," she said. "That's not what I was saying, at all."

"It's okay, you don't have to lie."

"I'm not lying, I would be fucked if you moved out all of a sudden," she said. "I can't afford—"

"You're just being nice," I said.

"I'm not! Can you stop for a second and *listen*—"

A wave of nausea passed over me, and this time I knew there was no amount of stillness that would cause it to pass. I yanked open the door and puked over the railing, into the bushes. Jojo came onto the landing and put her hand on my back.

"Are you okay?" she said.

I spit the sourness out of my mouth and, after several moments, turned to look at her. She was disgusted by the vomit, I could tell, but I saw, too, a flicker of genuine concern. I felt my chin wobbling.

"You're so pretty," I said.

She pursed her lips and swallowed, like I'd said the worst thing, then cupped my shoulder.

"Get some rest," she said. "We'll talk more tomorrow, okay?"

Chapter 6

I awoke in the foggy haze of morning. I had hardly slept and was still half submerged in my dream. It had been raining in Vienna. The rain was gothic, the monstrous buildings looming over slick streets. My dream-self had felt awful, so I'd gone out for a drink. I'd forgotten my umbrella, and as I walked the rain grew from a drizzle to a downpour. My jeans and T-shirt stuck to me, my hair became seaweed, rain pounded the crown of my head. Birds swooped off the bare trees in arcs, their wingbeats amplified by the rain. Most times this acute kind of sadness made me panic, but I sank into it, finding a richness there.

The café was grimy, dark, overly warm, with too many tables and walls covered with magazine clippings and posters. At the bar, a thin, tall man with a pert mustache moved languorously.

"Could I borrow a towel?" I stretched out my forearms, which dripped onto the bar. My hair streamed in rivulets. He stared at me with contempt as he wiped the counter underneath, jostling my arms, before he handed me the now-dirty dishrag.

At a corner table, I wrung my hair out into the dishtowel. All around, people were leaning in toward each other, talking with varying levels of boisterousness, eating cake and sipping espressos even though it was already night. I slouched into my chair.

"Yes, what you want," asked the waiter.

"Red wine and Sacher torte," I said.

He scribbled onto his pad and turned toward the table next to me, people he apparently knew. They shared some words in German and exploded in laughter.

I turned away, staring now at a woman a few tables away, her thinning hair dyed a putrid red. She chewed big bites of her own Sacher torte, flecks of chocolate flicking out at her companion as she spoke. Her scalp shone through what looked like sparse implants. I looked away in disgust, stared at the safe sight of my ragged fingernails.

The waiter clanked my wine onto the table without looking at me. *"Danke schön,"* I said to his retreating form. I took a big gulp, and wine dribbled onto my chin—I wiped it quickly with my hand, then looked around. No one had noticed. I took another sip, felt my scalp melt.

The Sacher torte arrived. I took another sip of wine first on my empty stomach, to feel the rancid pleasure of it and the swift little ache in the temples, before I sank my fork in. I dunked the bite into the pile of *schlag* alongside it and chewed the dry cake, then ran my tongue along my teeth, worrying the spaces in between, where microbits of cake had taken up residence.

My table shook as a man wedged himself between it and the one alongside, trying to get to the seat against the wall. He had a beard, thick as a forest; he had eyes like outer space. I slid my table over, making room for him. He sank into the chair next to me and I felt his heat, wanted to shift over and press my arm against his. Now he reached into his pocket for a handkerchief, which he passed over his face and then down over his beard, that lush crop of hair. He took out a notebook and pen and began scribbling, hunched over his writing.

"Writing anything good?"

The man continued to scribble. He probably spoke only German.

"You know who you look like?" I said.

He paused his pen and looked at me: those eyes. "I know who I am."

In retreading my dream, I'd come fully awake, and now I took in the details of my surroundings. The radiator, its interlocking carved shapes; the wooden dresser; the streaked mirror; the small window above my bed; the cheap curtains fanning out above me—my room. Brooklyn.

I was still wearing my shirt-dress. I was cold. There was an ache at the top of my skull—no wonder I'd been drinking in the dream. My mouth was mossy and dry. "Hello," I said to the room, testing out my voice, which emerged deep and crackly from my chest, the upper register dissolved.

I took yesterday's inventory, dredging images from the swamp: Dominic's condemning glare, a drink, patio guy, gravel piercing my knees, I'd been bad, his turned-away face, his disgust, *I saw you*, another drink, Celeste's party, dragging Jojo into the corner, my nails digging into her arm, I'd been bad, drinks and more drinks, Sam upstairs, *harder*, his hands in my hair, I'd been bad, *You don't give a shit what I want*, I would need to atone, my parents' apartment, *That's very short*, I was disgusting, Langham, his stony look of *no*, Jojo, right before bed, glaring at me from the staircase, I had treated Sam like shit, Sam, whom she loved, whom she cared about more than anyone, more than me—but before that, the bar, Freud. *Aren't you curious?* he had said, and *I know who I am,* or was that my dream?

I tried to reconstruct our conversation, but my mind had sucked much of it back up like quicksand. I remembered him smoking outside the bar, spotlit by the streetlight, the haze of smoke giving the image the sheen of a movie still. I remembered the scent of burning leaves hanging sharp in the air. I remembered him looking at me, *You came back,* that little smile. But then he had given me the minutest of headshakes. He had rejected me. The knowledge of this was acute and raw once more. He was better than me. But *Why do you need me to betray you?* he had asked, and *Come back,* he had said, and *Aren't you curious?*

I rose from bed slowly, trying not to jostle my brain inside my skull, and tested how I felt. My head was pounding, but my stomach felt solid, at least for now. In the mirror on top of my dresser, my lips were bright pink, my cheeks flushed, as they often were after I'd been drinking. I looked pretty.

I snuck to the bathroom and back, determined not to wake Jojo, and, safely returned to my room, beheld my shirt drawer. I had too many shirts, collected them like skins of a different self. There was the black mesh shirt, under which I'd wear my black bra, or even the bright red one, when I wanted to be noticed. There was the T-shirt I'd gotten at a thrift store, printed with an image of a candy bar from my childhood, which I wore out in Brooklyn. There was the avocado-colored shirt my father had given me long ago, a memento from a conference in California. I remembered him giving it to me, on the breast pocket a small patch with the name and logo of the store. The shirt was too small now, but I couldn't bear to give it away, though I never took it out of the drawer unless I got hammered and got the idea to try it on—or, on one mortifying occasion, to sleep with it tucked into the crook of my arm. I had no closet, only the hand-me-down dresser. My good shirts, all three, were hung in Jojo's closet; she had the bigger room. I would, I realized, need to get one before school on Monday—tomorrow. I could sneak back in tonight; maybe by then she'd have a chance to cool down—but *Why do you need me to betray you?* Was Jojo really enraged? I tried to recall what she'd said, her tone, and realized I could not. All I knew was the sour feeling deep in my stomach: fear, maybe, or mortification. Maybe by evening she'd have left for her boyfriend's, as she often did on Sunday nights.

As I rifled through the shirts, my mother's closet edged back into my mind. My desire to curl up underneath her clothes like a puppy. Wearing her pants—her "slacks." How ludicrous they had looked on me; they had only highlighted how pathetic I was. But better the slacks than what they covered, my legs, my self—even Langham hadn't wanted me!—Langham!—and now, flashing into focus, my father standing in the doorframe, *That's very short.* Shame bubbled up in me again. I grabbed the red cotton T-shirt with a big pocket on the breast, a high crew neck, so soft—the shirt I wore when I wanted to look bold while remaining hidden—and pulled on the jeans from yesterday. Freud would help me; Freud would save me.

My phone buzzed, the screen shone with a text from my mother:

Call when you can.

I turned it off, grabbed my jacket and a protein bar to eat on the way, and quickly, I left.

The bar looked both familiar and strange; I'd seen these lights dozens of times before, stretching up the walls, and yet—had they always been this rich amber hue? Had the bar always had this particular shine? I remembered sitting in that seat right near the corner—brown leather, not red, as it had been coded in my mind. Could it have been only yesterday? *I saw you*, Freud had said, and patio guy flashed into my mind. I looked furtively around the bar, but no, he wasn't here. No patio guy, no Dominic, no nobody. Just me, and Ed, and—soon—Freud.

Before Ed could speak to me, before he could even see me, I snuck out to a narrow hallway that ran alongside one wall of the bar. I'd peered down it a few times, curious what lay behind the door at the end. What else could it be but Freud? I walked along the hallway, growing high with anticipation.

The door was open a crack, and I could make out Freud, lying almost supine in his chair, feet propped on the desk in front of him, head cocked to the side. I knocked. He licked the tip of his middle finger and used it to dog-ear the page of his book, which he closed and placed on the desk. He removed his reading glasses and placed them on top of the book, then finally rose out of the chair and made his way toward the door. At his approach, I began to sweat.

My jacket was overwarm for the morning. I fiddled with the napkin, still in my pocket; it was beginning to disintegrate under my fingers' constant probing. Had he meant *come back whenever you want*? Or had he just meant *come back one time*? But he had said it again last night, hadn't he, when I'd left the bar—or had I imagined that? I hadn't taken the napkin out and looked at it in hours and wondered with a hit of panic whether his words were still etched there. I thought about leaving, but he was three feet away, now two, now one, now creaking open the office door. He looked impassive, neither delighted nor disappointed, impressed nor unimpressed, and definitely not surprised.

"Good morning," he said. "Come in."

He stood aside and I entered, took in the room: cozy, full of books on wooden shelves with glass-paned doors, an armchair, a low broad couch. A small window looked out onto a tree, just beginning to turn. There was an intricate old rug covering the wood floor. Antiques everywhere. One, hung on the wall, was a bas-relief of a woman walking, her robes flowing around her. There was a painting of a woman, half fainted against the man behind her, who propped her up in his arms. Another man stood next to them, lecturing to a roomful of note-taking spectators, all men in suits, as though she were a specimen for study. They were doctors, perhaps; I wondered what had befallen her. Beneath the painting was Freud's desk chair, odd and even unsightly: a curved semicircle of wooden armrest supported only by a padded bar running down from the middle.

"It was designed by a friend, to suit my reading habits," he said.

"And they let you bring it in here?"

"Why not?"

I glanced at him and in a rush remembered pushing him last night—the firmness of his chest, his hand on my wrist. I felt the twist between my legs—*fuck me*—then, swiftly, the shame—*If you sleep with me, you'll have to dispose of me*—my men, being poured down the drain, shredded to oblivion—

I felt dizzy. I closed my eyes. My dad standing in the doorway, *That's very short*, the garish carpet, a nauseous swell—

"Could I lie down?" I said.

He gestured toward the couch, then sank into the arm-chair behind it.

The couch was good. It wasn't hard enough to feel like an affront, nor did it threaten to swallow me. Minutes passed. The ringing in my ears began to subside. There was a blanket, folded, at the end, and I put my feet on top of it, shoes still on. It wasn't at all muddy outside, it was a crisp and dry day, but I liked the thought that there might be a clod of dirt on the soles of my shoes that would re-main on the blanket whenever I left, if I ever left. Residue of me. From this angle the slats of the blinds blocked out the view; the room was a brown cocoon.

I thought I heard a murmur from the bar beyond the door, but it was hard to tell; he had a fan whirring and it blocked out much of the noise. I had taken off my jacket before I'd lain down, so now I was in just my T-shirt. I crossed my arms over my chest like a mummy. The napkin was far from me—but it didn't matter anymore, because Freud was here. Watching me. He sat behind me, completely still. I couldn't even hear him breathe.

"Are you still there?" I asked.

"I'm here."

"Can I pull the blanket up over me?"

"Yes."

Why did he want me to come back? Why, if he didn't want to fuck me? *Aren't you curious?* But I wanted Freud to touch me, I wanted him to put his hands on my face, my forehead, his warm palms radiating through my mind—

Was that such a horrible thing to want? What if that was all I asked for? *Just touch me,* I silently begged. *Put your hands on my face. Forget about fucking, just touch; please, put your hands on my face—*

And then, just like that, he did. His fingers splayed over my eyebrows. His palms pressed into the crown of my head.

"Say everything that comes to mind," he said.

"Everything?"

"Everything."

I relaxed into the pressure of his hands. I wanted him to press his fingertips, hard and harder, until my head hurt—no, I just wanted him to touch me, it was enough. The warmth of his palms on my scalp. His fingers on my forehead. I wished his fingerprints would leave marks, swirls and swirls across my skin. *Freud's hands are on my face,* I thought—and an image rose in me of the Metropolitan Opera House, its five arches stretching up like fingers, each one etched with a series of interlocking glass panes.

"The first time I came was at the opera," I said.

My stomach lurched, and I went silent. Could I really tell Freud about touching myself as a little girl? If I started, what else would I say? But I had already begged him to fuck me, it wasn't like he didn't know—and yet that was different, wasn't it, from telling him what had happened in the opera house bathroom, so long ago.

"What do you remember?"

"I'm afraid to say," I said. "Afraid I'll say too much."

"Start small," he said. "Just tell me about where you were."

"It was in the bathroom," I said, "right as the opera was about to end."

The show was *Werther*, I told him; my parents had brought me. Since the first moment Werther had entered the stage, hunched forward, I had been transfixed—his face a series of sharp edges, framed by thick dark hair swooping back; his body tilted forward, like a fox in flight. Whenever he'd turned, his long black coat had whipped behind him, and I'd caught a glimpse of his ass in tight tan pants: two orbs, catching the light. His *ass*—I'd first overheard one of the sports boys say the word at school and had been repeating it to myself for weeks. By that point in the show, Werther's obsession, Charlotte—who was engaged to another man—had rejected him for the final time, sending him into an anguished frenzy. As he writhed on the stage, his cloak sliced through the air, and I saw flashes of his body beneath, white shirt straining this way and that across his chest.

Now, on the couch, recounting the scene for Freud, a pulsing began to build between my legs, just as it had in the opera house seat. I was young, but I had been visited by this second little heartbeat before—like when I'd watched the boys at school shove each other on the playground, or when I'd seen a boy on the beach, hunched forward, his rib cage like bat wings, and imagined what the bones would feel like on my palm, moving beneath his skin. *Or,* I thought without speaking, *when I first saw you.* I wouldn't tell him about the book cover, not now. I couldn't bear it if he didn't understand, if he said anything other than: *That was me.* But did I even need to tell him? Didn't he already know? Didn't he know everything? I couldn't remember which had come first—the book or the opera, Freud or Werther. They had the same effect—that mysterious pulsing, pleasurable and frightening at once. *My vagina is sick,* I thought in those moments. This I told Freud. I'd sat on my foot as I always did, digging my heel into my crotch, to make the pulsing recede. Onstage, Werther had reached a decision: without Charlotte's love, he could not continue to live. I read the words on the screen built into the seat in front of me as he sang them: "CHARLOTTE HAS DECREED MY SENTENCE. OPEN MY TOMB!"

I paused in my recollection, so long that Freud gently asked, "And then?"

"When I had that... feeling," I said, referring to the pulsing, "I thought maybe I needed to—" *To pee,* I was about to say. "To go to the bathroom."

I had hurried out of the auditorium, I told Freud, side-stepping along the row of seats, all those middle-aged knees. I could feel my father's gaze burning into my back, reproaching me, but I kept speed walking, my shoes thudding on the carpet, past the usher and along the hallway and by the water fountain and through the bathroom door.

The stalls had been empty save for the first, where a woman in orthopedic shoes blew her nose loudly. "*Psssssss*," I heard her say, beckoning the pee, and after a moment there was the responsive tinkle. I walked fast to the far end and put toilet paper on the seat and tried to squeeze out some pee myself, but I could hardly do so, it was so swollen. I reached my fingers down to touch the hot sleek pillow, and this felt good, like some relief. The woman flushed and moved to the sink, I pulled the skirt of my dress farther up my legs and continued to press my fingers inside as an image of Werther, clutching his head, floated before me. The woman washed her hands, the door swung closed behind her, I continued to press into the softness until it began to clench and unclench and clench and unclench and a raw yelp escaped from somewhere deep inside. The sound bounced back from the walls of the bathroom stall.

"By the time I returned to my seat," I said, "Werther had died, and the opera was over."

Freud's hands were still on my forehead. I felt sudden panic that, in recounting the story, I'd begun to touch myself—had I? I grabbed for the top of my pants underneath the blanket and found them still buttoned. My fingertips were dry. Okay.

But I had wanted to.

Could I?

No. *Stop*.

"What was it about Werther that so aroused you?" Freud said, interrupting.

"It was..." But I couldn't say. Not because I was withholding something, but because I didn't know. The only thing

I could think was: *His ass.* And also: *Maybe he reminded me of you.* "I don't know," I said, and after that I didn't speak.

Minutes of silence. Then Freud spoke.

"Did your parents often bring you to the opera?" he said. He was coaxing me. I would be coaxed.

"No," I replied. "That was the first time."

They went somewhere every Saturday night, I told him—this was before they'd begun their tradition of hosting weekly dinners—and would leave me at home to eat microwaved meals with the sitter. They went to dinner, to the theater, to a lecture, to visit colleagues—and, sometimes, to the opera. On these occasions, they would listen to the sound track all week in preparation, and I'd be alternately entranced and repulsed by the voices streaming out of the speaker. Mostly, I tried not to listen, because doing so would make me think too much about the moment they would leave. I always stood at the window after they'd walked out the door, in a cloud of my mother's perfume, looking down at the street below, waiting for their tiny heads to emerge from under the awning of our building. I would watch them hail a cab. I would watch this dollhouse version of my father open the door for my mother. I would watch her delicately lift her dress to step inside and my father step in after her. Then the door would close, and the cab would leave, and I would strain at the window until I could no longer see the taxi's two bright red eyes.

That particular Saturday, I was given a dress and told to put it on. I was going to join them. When I found out, just hours before, I was flooded with an excitement so intense it felt like terror. Now it was my tiny head ducking

113

into the car. I was so overcome with emotion as we got into the taxi that I wanted to scream. I looked up toward the windows of our tall building, reflecting the sunset, as if to tell the ghost of me standing there, *I've made it.*

"What would she have said?" Freud asked. "The ghost of you?"

"She would have said, *Calm down.*" A warning.

My father had told me to calm down when I was in these moods so often that by this point I'd learned to say it to myself. After one temper tantrum, he had given me a rubber band to put on my wrist and instructed me to snap it against my skin when I felt on the verge of the next flood of emotion. Was I wearing a rubber band that night? I couldn't remember. I did remember thinking those words—*calm down*—as I looked out the window of the taxi. The city rushed past, red neon bleeding into yellow into green into blue. A mother, bent forward, pushed a stroller, tendrils of her hair floating in the summer breeze. The sky was orange feathers. Two parents took their child between them, one hand each, and swung him high over the sidewalk. His laugh ricocheted off my window.

Calm down, I told myself, *calm down.*

The Metropolitan Opera House rose shimmering into the twilit sky. There were its five arches. In the dark of impending night, a chandelier shone through the center pane; on the edges, in the arches that made up the building's pinkie and thumb, two bold tapestries beamed out into the evening. At once, the fountain in front of the building shot upward, a sharp jubilant spray of light. In my memory, a little girl stood silhouetted before it, her feet planted wide, her arms thrown into a V, the black lines of her small body making a snow angel in the expansive summer night.

"Is that what you wanted to do?" Freud said.

"Yes," I said, and in the moment the word took shape, I felt a stunned certainty that the little girl had never existed. There she had always been in my memory—her silhouette, bold and free, as I walked beside my parents. But—

"I have this strange feeling I've imagined her," I said to Freud.

"Why?" He shifted behind me, but his hands remained in place. I pushed my head into them; he pushed back, holding me in.

"Because that's exactly what I wanted to do."

I wanted to run up to the fountain and throw my arms wide, holler into the air. The centers of my palms itched with anticipation and I made fists, scratching my palms with my fingernails, trying to contain myself. My shoes clicked on the concrete. My parents, walking right next to me, felt far away. *Let me go!* I thought. *Let me explode!* I wished to grab their hands and have them swing me back and forth, back and forth, like that boy on the sidewalk, then shoot me like a catapult over the bursting white fountain and right into the palm of the building, beckoning me toward it, waiting to catch me.

"And what would that have meant?" Freud asked. "To be caught—to be held?"

For reasons I didn't understand, tears sprang to my eyes. I shook my head briskly, trying to make him release me, but his hands remained.

"Fuck this," I said. "Let me go."

But he didn't. He smoothed his thumbs over my eyebrows, a tenderness that caused me to flush.

"You can cry," he said.

I shook my head, then shoved my head backward into his hands like an angry mare, as if to hurt him. He traced my eyebrows again, refusing.

"I'm scared," I said.

"What are you afraid of?" he said.

I didn't answer. Instead, in response to his gentle tone, my mind returned to the scene. I took a series of steady breaths, and once I was certain I would not cry, I spoke.

"On the way into the auditorium, we met Patrice, a friend of my parents' from graduate school, and her husband," I said. "I just saw them last night." They'd had their son, Leroy, with them, the one who had been skipping dinners for a long time. Telling Freud, I realized it had been years, at least, since I'd conjured the image of our mothers standing behind us, their hands on our shoulders. Patrice was composed, tall and thin in a sleek knee-length red dress, but nothing like my mother, whose simple floor-length black gown only highlighted the beauty of her face, her blue-green eyes.

"It smells here," Leroy whispered to me as our parents' voices arced over us.

I sniffed and scrunched up my nose, then flapped my hand in front of my face to make him laugh. He did, so I flapped harder. My mother's fingers tightened around my collarbones.

"We're joking," I said.

She leaned down, her soft cheek brushing mine. I could smell her face cream, a sweet green scent. Her necklace, a delicate chain, grazed the crook of my neck, making me shiver.

"Strike one," she whispered.

Leroy was still watching me. I couldn't tell if he had heard. I tried to smile at him, as though everything were still fine, but my mouth must have done something else, because he was looking at me with fear.

My mother's hands loosened their grip, then released me. The shoulders of my dress were two cold spots from the moisture her palms had left behind. She touched Patrice's arm and they all turned to go inside. I followed. I was cold and small in the drafty expanse, and crossed my arms tight.

"Strike one," Freud echoed.

"Yes," I said.

"Did she say that often?"

"Yes."

"How many strikes were there?"

"Three."

"And then?"

"I never got to three."

I had never asked what would happen if I did. With my father, the punishment was immediate and swift, with no warning. With my mother, it was a threat. I didn't know which I preferred: the unanticipated shock, or the looming possibility of unknown disaster.

"Immediate and swift," said Freud, "such as—"

"Stop pushing me!" I said, too loudly, shocking myself. My throat had gone tight, my mind cloudy.

Freud didn't respond.

I had the urge to grab his wrist, dig my nails into his arm—Jojo, her scared, fierce face—my eyes grew hot and wet and I reached up toward Freud's hands but I didn't grab him, I didn't claw him, I laced my fingers between his and lifted his hands off my scalp and just held them, held his hands.

"You need to let go," he said, and gently released my hands, then placed his palms on my forehead once more.

"Hold me," I whimpered.

"You want me to take away your discomfort."

"Yes!" I said.

"But discomfort is where we begin."

Long minutes of silence.

"Are you still there?" I asked.

"I'm here."

"Do you want me to keep telling you the story?"

"Why do you think you asked me that question?"

"Because I want you to beg me," I said.

"You want me to care."

"Yes."

"I care."

In the auditorium, I told him, I was seated next to my father, with my mother on his other side. Seats stretched around us in a sweep of red velvet. We were in the front row of the balcony; people sat in boxes below us and in long curves along the sides of the room. They looked cozy, ensconced in their pods, waiting for the show to begin. Usually, when the three of us sat together, my mother positioned herself between us, but because we'd come with the Lyles, my mother now sat next to Patrice. I was jittery at the opportunity to sit near my dad for the hours of the production. I shifted my body closer to his, not quite brushing his arm. His body was angled just slightly toward my mother's. He parted his hair on the left; I could see the bare skin between the sections of dark brown. It had a sheen to it, as if he had scrubbed in between the two sections of hair with a scratchy sponge. It was the straightest part I'd ever seen, the hair branching out from it like Moses's sea. I longed to touch it, that bright line, to feel the tidy hair grazing the tip of my finger from both sides.

My mother whispered something to him. I watched as his left eye crinkled at the corner. I remembered the crinkle with such precision, and the sharp tug it elicited inside me—I wanted desperately to know what they had said. But I didn't interrupt. I looked down: my hands sat barren, holding each other. My mother had made me wear a blue dress with a waist that pinched. It felt too young for me, and my hands, surrounded by the blueness poufing from my lap, looked ridiculous. My mother laughed, an ethereal sound.

I peered over the railing into the orchestra, speckled with gray and brown and black and blond and also shiny heads, gaps of plush red where people hadn't shown up. The room felt too big to me, an abyss that would dissolve me if I let it, like salt in hot water. I could have sat in one of those seats, next to another girl, alone with her parents, too. She would love grapes as much as I did, would love peeling off the skin in thin filaments, finally biting off each end and sucking out the middle to make a tiny, squishy doughnut. We would each squint an eye and look at each other through our empty grapes, and we would giggle so high and hard the opera would tell us to be quiet.

The lights dimmed. The gold curtain parted. A group of children in colorful dresses and shorts entered from a stone house, nestled among the trees, and began to sing. A man sang back. The voices pulsed through the room, raw as muscle tendons. It was nothing like it had been on the speaker. The hairs rose up along my forearms, my shins, my thighs, my scalp. I couldn't tell if I wanted to clamp my hands over my ears and squeeze my eyes closed or lean so close I could melt into those trembling notes. Both, at once.

"What's happening?" I whispered to my father.

He raised one finger and arched his eyebrows, his way of saying, *Aha!* Then he reached across me to that rectangular screen on the back of the seat I faced, his forearm grazing my skin. I stared at his pointer finger as he pressed the button, the black hairs curling toward his knuckle.

"What is it?" I said, to make him stay near.

"Watch," he whispered, sending warmth through my right ear and through my skull and down my neck and arms.

The screen lit up with red capital letters, translating the voices.

"It's new," my dad whispered, gesturing to the box.

"Cool!" I said—but he put his finger to his lips, then angled his body away again. I stared at the two of them, just barely making out my mother's face in the darkness, the lovely angle of her cheekbone highlighted in the light from the stage, her eyes in shadow. My dad, sensing my gaze on them, looked over at me, his eyes glowing like a cat's, and jutted his chin toward the stage.

Into the emptiness entered Werther—his thick dark hair, the two spheres of his ass flashing from beneath his coat. *Ass, ass, ass*, I whispered to myself—my throat went tight, and I swallowed so loudly I was certain the whole room could hear. I turned toward my father and laid my head on his shoulder. I tried to telegraph that I wanted him to reach around me and squeeze my shoulder or smooth my hair or lay his head upon mine.

"To telegraph?" Freud said.

"To ask him without having to speak," I said, thinking he didn't know the word in English. But that wasn't what he meant.

"Why didn't you ask him?" he said. "Why do you think you needed him to read your mind?"

"Because I knew already," I said, and my throat caught.

"You knew what?"

"I knew he didn't want to touch me."

"How did you know?"

"I've always known."

I'd learned this as a child. The first time I could remember was crawling into his lap, picture book splayed open next to us, my thumb in my mouth. He had pushed me off, onto the couch, so quickly it was as if by reflex. "Sit *next* to Daddy," he'd said, patting my knee, *tap-tap*.

I had tried never to break the rule. But there, in the opera, insane and drunk off the music, off my searing aloneness, I couldn't help myself and let my ear graze the shoulder of his suit jacket. I willed myself to stop, *Sit* next *to Daddy*, told myself to lift my head, lift it!—but *Touch me*, I said in my mind, unable to make myself budge an inch, hoping if I thought it loudly enough, he would hear. I needed him to hear me. I needed him to touch me; I needed him to read my mind. It wasn't impossible; there were those rare moments he placed his hand on my neck. It could happen, if just for a moment. But he sat still, like a plank of wood. My neck began to cramp; I realized I hadn't relaxed onto his shoulder, I was just resting my head lightly, not wanting to burden him with the weight of it. Finally, I lifted it back up and sank into my seat.

"And how did you feel?" Freud asked.

"Like I wanted to die," I said, though until the words had left my mouth, I hadn't known they were true.

Werther, onstage, was experiencing the same anguish. Moments earlier, he had declared his love for Charlotte in his chocolate-mousse voice—"MY HEART IS FILLED WITH DELIGHT. WHAT A DREAM, TO BE CRADLED BY HER GAZE..." My insides had felt pumped through with liquid metal at this betrayal: Werther was supposed to be *mine*. My loneliness was unbearable. But then Charlotte's father had entered to announce that her fiancé had returned. Werther clutched his head in despair, just as I wished to do: "REMAIN LOYAL TO YOUR OATH, CHARLOTTE—BUT I WILL DIE OF IT!" His pain rippled through the room.

In the seats, I'd closed my eyes. A high-pitched ringing sounded in my ears, almost drowning out what was happening onstage. In my mind I fixed on the image of Werther, crying out, clutching his head. It made me hot and excited, uncontainable. I imagined running up onto the stage and threading my arms underneath his long black coat and around his waist. My cheek soft against his stomach. He would put his big arms around me, curve his tall body over mine. Remembering this, I became aroused on the couch again—my eyes sprang open. Could Freud tell? I swallowed loud and dry.

"What are you thinking?" he prodded.

"You can tell," I said, "can't you?"

"You tell me," he said, his voice low and suggestive to my ears. I got wetter.

"Are you sure you won't fuck me?" I whispered.

"Fucking is escape," he said.

"Can't I escape?"

"Do you want to?" he said. "Or are you curious?"

It was a test. I would be curious.

"One must seek to learn something from everything," Freud said.

I paused for a long time, waiting for the pulsation in my crotch to subside. I squeezed tight the muscles there, willing the sensation away. I allowed my mind to float back to the scene, the velvet seats, Werther's despair and mine...

"What else do you remember?" Freud prodded.

"I remember the intermission," I said.

When the lights came up, I'd peered into the orchestra down below. It was dark, but I could still make out the tiny heads. A kid reached up and patted his dad on the top of his head; the father grasped the kid's forearm and I winced. But he brought the little hand to his mouth and kissed its palm, then blew raspberries into it, making his son laugh. I felt a hand on my forearm and saw that my mother, stretching across my father's lap, was handing me a butterscotch candy. She pointed at her cheeks, hollowed out with sucking, and raised her eyebrows: she knew they were my favorite. Maybe she was apologizing for her tone earlier, with the Lyles, I reasoned, or maybe she was rewarding me for my compliance. Or maybe she just loved me the most, my mom. I took it from her elegant fingers and unwrapped it.

"*Shh,*" she said.

"Sorry," I whispered. My cheeks burned. I slouched into the seat and sucked hard on the butterscotch. My dress itched my thighs, and I pulled my knees into my chest. I crunched on the butterscotch and it broke in two, and I pressed the jagged pieces with my tongue into the roof of my mouth, then listened as my parents talked with the Lyles. Patrice, like both of my parents, was a therapist, I told Freud, and when they were together they talked about work.

"Your parents are therapists?"

"Yes," I said. That was where the rubber band idea had come from: it was one of their techniques. They worked out of the apartment next door, I told him. I would sit alone, doing my homework in our apartment after school, imagining all sorts of things going on just beyond the wall. I hated their clients; I wanted to know everything about them. So when they spoke about their patients in front of me, I tried to disappear.

Leroy had sat between his parents, and as his mother spoke, he leaned back into his father, who draped his arm around Leroy and patted his stomach. He sucked his thumb, something he seemed much too old for. Then he leaned forward, away from the pillow of his father's body, and looked at me.

"Psst," he said.

I gave a brisk shake of my head, trying to keep listening to my parents.

"Opera is so *boring*," he whispered. "Right?"

I looked away from him, out into the orchestra. In the aisle, a tall woman stood in a long velvet dress, her sharp shoulders jutting out from the straps. Her companion was much shorter than she, a stubby and balding man, but they fit together, her effervescence shining onto him and his plainness grounding her.

"Right?" Leroy said again. "Isn't it *boring*?"

I ignored him. I didn't think the opera was boring at all. I thought it was devastating.

"Devastating," Freud echoed.

"Yes."

"How so?"

"Werther loved her!" I said, my voice catching unexpectedly. "He loved her and he couldn't have her..." Saying the words, I felt my chest go tight, the same feeling I'd had the day before, on the back patio, the feeling that had made me desperate for the man with the cigarette. I needed to fuck someone now, I needed it, if I didn't I might die, I might explode—

"What are you thinking?" Freud said, but I could only shake my head beneath his palms.

Many minutes of silence.

Finally Freud spoke again. "He couldn't have her, just as you couldn't have your father."

"That's disgusting," I said quickly. *Do you mean I can't have you?* Werther's odes of horrible sorrow played again in my mind. Charlotte's voice was high and screeching, it drilled into the top of my skull; but Werther's slid straight down my throat and through my chest and into my stomach, where it made a red-hot home. He was in agony. Again and again, from my perch above the orchestra, I imagined running toward him on the stage, threading my arms under his long black coat; he would wrap it around the back of my head, press me to him, press his hard stomach back into me. He would hide me, swallow me, no one would even know I was there. Pricks of pain burned along my thighs; I was digging my nails into the skin.

I remembered looking up at my dad, who stared impassively at the stage. On impulse, I touched my finger to the front of his part and dragged it down the length of his head. He shuddered, then turned to me, his face a map of repulsion. I had already retracted my bad hand, was hugging it to me.

"I did not like that," he whispered, his voice like sandpaper. But why? Why didn't he like the feel of my finger on his head? Why hadn't he laid his head on mine when I'd rested on his shoulder, making a sandwich? He didn't, he wouldn't, he couldn't.

"I'm sorry," I whispered back. "It looked shiny..."

He squinted at me, breathing through widened nostrils, then turned back toward the stage, where Werther was making arrangements to leave the town. My organs seemed to shrivel. If I'd thought Werther was full of desire when he'd entered the stage, he was now exploding with it, his movements grand and beseeching. He was going to go away, yes—but now he was bellowing out into the hall that he wanted to end his life.

"And that was when I ran to the bathroom," I said to Freud.

I waited for Freud to make a pronouncement, but he just sat in silence, his palms still arcing across my head. So much time passed that I began to grow drowsy, wondered if perhaps I would drift off to sleep.

"Why did you tell me that story?" he asked finally.

The shame swept up into my face. His words echoed in my mind, becoming more savage with each reverberation: *Why did you tell me that story? Disgusting—a story about you diddling yourself at the opera? —really? —*

"You said to say whatever came to mind!" It was something about his hands, which were still on my forehead—his hands, the opera house, its five fingers—I grabbed his wrist and pulled it toward me, stuck his finger in my mouth. I had expected it to taste dirty, like after his bar shift, but there was just the faintest bitterness in the middle of my tongue.

"Let go."

"No," I said, forming the word around his finger, and pressed my teeth into his knuckle. He didn't make a sound. I wound my tongue around his finger, round and round, the thick hairs grazing the underside of my tongue, which was so tender.

"Why are you doing this?" he said.

"You don't like it?"

"You need to think about *why*," he said. "Isn't that the reason you're here?"

I inched the finger out of my mouth, scraping my teeth along it, but when I got to the nail I bit down.

Freud yelped. I laughed.

"Finally!" I said. "Finally!"

"Finally what?" he said.

"Finally, I win," I said, "me!"

"What did you win?"

"I won your pain."

I had meant to say "attention." I could have said a thousand words that didn't make me sick, but "pain" was not one of them.

"That isn't what you want."

My hand was still on his wrist. He had removed his other hand from my forehead and seemed to have placed it on the arm of the couch, behind me; he was trying to wrench himself away from me. I was still lying on my back and couldn't see him at all, just my forearm, hovering above my face. I would not let go. I pulled his arm toward me like a rope, alternating hand by hand: forearm, elbow, biceps. And now his face was above mine, upside down, such that I could barely read his expression. I wanted him to kiss me softly, in this upside-down way, like they did in the movies. I released one of my hands and jammed my fingers through the underside of his beard, yanking him toward me. His lips were pursed tight. I had the sense that I could open my mouth wide enough to swallow him whole. I pictured it: my mouth stretching into a chasm, pulling him into me, first his head, his beard scratching my throat, then his shoulders, his arms like spaghetti... Everything he'd ever said would be inside me. *Did you want to be seen?* But then I'd be all alone. He would have nothing more to say.

I released him.

Silence.

"Put your hands on my head again," I said, but he didn't respond. "Do it!"

"It's not a good idea," he said.

"Please!" I said.

As if he had read my mind: "If you eat me up, there will be nothing left."

More silence.

"What are you doing?" Freud asked, and I realized that I had been probing the roof of my mouth with my tongue again.

"It's something I do to calm myself," I told him. "I run my tongue along the roof of my mouth. But recently it became ruined—I noticed it felt too much like something else..."

"Like what?"

"I can't say."

"Why not?"

"I'm afraid it will remind you of what you saw yesterday, in the back of the bar." I was afraid—and I wanted it. I wanted him to know everything. But didn't he already?

"It reminds you of a penis," he said.

Penis. "Dick," "cock," "prick," even "wang"—I'd call it anything but a "penis." It sounded too vulnerable, like a baby animal. I soundlessly carved the word into the air with my lips, trying it out—*penis, penis*—and, as I did so, images from yesterday coursed through me: Dominic's sneer, patio guy, grabbing Jojo's arm, Sam's rejection and Langham's, too, my father, *That's very short*—I squeezed my eyes shut, trying to stall the tape as it ribboned through my mind. *Come back.* What had he asked me? My tongue, my mouth. *It reminds you of a—*

"Yes," I said. "It reminds me of a... *penis*." But why, I wondered, would the fact that the inside of a mouth reminded me of a dick make it any less of a home? Weren't dicks the only thing I loved?

"Why did you tell me that story?" he said again, and again there was the helpless flood of rage. It occurred to me there was nothing keeping me in this position. I grabbed the arm of the couch and clawed myself around to face him. There he was. I stayed on my belly, my chin resting on the arm of the couch.

"You will obey me," I said.

He didn't respond, but there was a glint in his eyes that thrilled me—wasn't there?—and my heart raced. The image of him I'd had as a child: me draped over his lap, his hand grabbing my hair, wrenching my head around, the other hand smacking my ass—in a second, I was wet. Would he really do it—would he pull me onto his lap, would he spank me? I was dizzy, I was thrilled, either this would happen or I would faint—

"You know what I want," I said.

He was silent, just looking at me.

"Spank me."

More silence. More looking.

"Spank me!"

Silence.

"Then let me fuck you!"

"You don't really want to do that."

"Why is everyone always telling me what I do and don't want?"

He didn't respond. A little whimper, the beginning of a tantrum, bubbled out of me.

"I need to touch myself," I whispered.

He didn't speak or move. I pulled myself over the arm of the couch so that it pressed into my stomach. With every move I made, I stared harder into his eyes: as I reached underneath to unbutton my jeans; as I pulled them down over my ass; as I began smacking myself with my left hand while I touched myself with my right. His eyes bore into mine. I rubbed harder, harder. The couch pressed deeper into my belly. My left arm began to ache but I continued to smack myself, again and again and again. He barely moved, but I saw his heart beating at his neck. As I came, he watched me scream.

I continued to hold his gaze, panting deep in my throat. Then I slid back onto the couch, flipped myself back over, pulled my jeans back up, and lay in filled-up quiet.

"Why do you think you needed to do that?" he said.

Immediately I felt sick. The urge to masturbate again was almost unbearable. I didn't know how to answer and instead pulled the blanket back up to my chin and wrapped my arms around myself and closed my eyes.

"I'm sorry," I whispered.

"I am not criticizing you," he said. "I am asking you to examine."

"Is there a difference?"

"There is," he said. "There is all the difference in the world."

Underneath the blanket, so slowly I was sure he couldn't see, I slid my hand toward my crotch again, then pressed my fingers there. The intense comfort of it, my home.

"I've done it for a very long time," I said. "Like I told you."

Silence.

"I can't help it," I said finally.

"There is no need to help it," he said. "I am only suggesting that it might provide clues as to who you are."

People masturbate when they're full of craving, when they're horny, when they want. This much was obvious. But this wasn't all of it, I knew. I thought back to the opera, to what had happened right before I'd run to the bathroom: Werther, his anguished frenzy, my own.

"I masturbate when I feel lonely," I said.

"When you want to connect—" Freud softly said.

"When I feel so profoundly lonely, such intense longing, it seems insatiable."

"—and the connection isn't there to be had," he continued. "So instead, you connect with yourself."

I pressed my fingers harder over my pants, not rubbing myself, just holding myself in. When you come, you're in ecstasy; you leave yourself for a moment. *Little death.* You come, so you can come back to yourself.

"Yes," I whispered, and for some reason then was able to pull my hand away. "I'm remembering something..." I said. "What happened after the opera. Please, will you put your hands on my head?"

There they were again, palms pressing into my skull.

When we'd gotten home, I told him, my mother had gone to get ready for bed, while my father had gone to tidy the kitchen—there were still dinner dishes in the sink. I felt my cheeks still flushed from what had happened in the bathroom; I hadn't known my body could do that. I had felt the twisting there before, had rubbed and pressed my crotch in all sorts of ways, but never before had I ascended to that white-hot place.

I stood watching my father from the doorway, his hands covered in suds, his studied expression. He had taken off his jacket but was still in his suit pants, which hung in a long line to the floor.

I paused, unsure if I could continue. Freud had just watched me come, and yet what I had to say next felt like another order of revelation.

"I can't say what I need to say," I told him.

"Why?"

"I'm afraid."

No response.

"Are you still there?"

"I'm here," Freud said, and of course he was, I felt his hands on my hair.

I swallowed. I balled my shirt up in my fists. I opened them, slipped one hand underneath the waistband of my jeans and pressed my palm into my stomach, the soft hot skin.

"I couldn't stop looking at his ass," I blurted out, and then sighed deeply, relieved I had managed to let the words into the air, relieved I hadn't been struck dead. His ass had looked firm, tough, but like it had a little bit of spring to it. I'd never seen him naked, not even in his underwear, except when he was wearing a bathing suit. I'd never seen a man's ass at all, or a boy's. What shape was it? It was hard to tell through his clothes. Was it hairy, like his legs? What did it feel like?

I edged into the kitchen and then behind him, crouched down a little, laid my cheek on it. It was better than a pillow, even through his pants; I thought that word—*pillow*—as my cheek made contact. But just as my eyelids floated closed and an orange feeling spread through my chest, his body went rigid. I lifted myself away, slowly, willing my body to disappear into thin air. Maybe he hadn't noticed. Maybe I could transform myself into a ghost.

"What were you doing," my father said in a monotone, like it wasn't a question.

"I don't know," I whispered, which was true. He turned around. I stared at the floor, tiny gleaming white tiles.

"Look at me," he said.

I couldn't; my eyes were magnetized, the tiles like teeth.

"Look at me. Now."

I pulled my chin up and my eyes followed. His eyes were coin slots.

A laugh bubbled in my stomach. I tried to squash it down, but it slid out of my mouth in squeaks. My father grabbed the top of my arm with his fingers and dug them in, his nails burrowing into me, then whirled me back around toward the cabinets. There was the slap of my palms against the wood. Abruptly he released my arm. With one hand he yanked up the skirt of the dress; with the other one he spanked me. I was too stunned to cry. I didn't turn around, but I heard him walk away, out of the room.

I held the arm he'd grabbed away from me, his fingertips still pulsing on my biceps, my arm a poisoned thing. I stood with my legs apart, as if trying to give my ass as much air as possible; it was stinging. Finally I started to cry over the sink, my tears falling onto the still-dirty dishes. They understood me, I thought—my soiled friends. Finally I splashed some cold water on my face and went to bed.

When I had finished, Freud made a small noise—*mm*. A noise of sympathy. And then he was silent.

We sat that way for many moments. My heart thudded, loud and muddled, in my ears. My teeth were chattering, like my body didn't know what to do with the story I had just unleashed, and I'd spontaneously fallen ill.

"What does that story mean?" I said.

"What do you think?"

"I don't know..."

"You say you knew your father did not like to be touched," Freud said. "Why do you think you tried—again—to touch him?"

"You're blaming me?" I said. "*Me?* For my father hitting me?" My father had never mentioned it again. I tried to remember whether he'd ever hit me again, yet oddly, I could not. It didn't matter: what had seared itself into my mind was not just the spanking but the knowledge that the capacity for it was inside him. The capacity and the desire. That and the expression on his face, those narrowed eyes, full of rage. The next day, I remembered, he had been different: cautious in a way I found alarming, as though he were afraid of me.

"Blaming?" Freud said. "Do you hear me blaming—or do you hear me asking a question?"

"Blaming," I said, though I didn't even know if I meant it.

"Do you think it's possible," he said, "that you wanted your father to touch you so badly that you would do anything?"

Chapter 7

The session had ended so abruptly I felt drugged, my whole body humming like a tuning fork. I blinked into the outside light. The city looked strange, the way it does when you come back from vacation. Spots that had faded into invisibility stood out to me once more: the potted plants guarding the entrance to the bar; the brownstones across the street, families sandwiched inside; the tree sprouting out of the sidewalk. Its base was ringed by a quartet of leafy plants—how had I never noticed them before? A cat crept underneath the cars. He heard me moving and froze, fixed me with his bright eyes. Did he know what had just unfolded? It seemed unreal that only the night before, I had found Freud on this very corner, smoking in the hazy glow of the streetlamp, looking sublime. That only yesterday, he had come back into my life.

I was suddenly starving. Aside from the protein bar, I hadn't eaten all day. I thought of the burrito place, with its two lone tables, its green-and-yellow color scheme. It had always repulsed me, but now it seemed like the only thing that would fill me up.

I walked in a daze. I pictured Freud, staring at me as I slapped myself, touched myself, came; but it wasn't his eyes I conjured so much as that faint pulsation in his neck. The pulsation that meant we were alive together in my transgression. I felt my own pulse, thrumming hard at the memory—me, draped over the arm of the couch; Freud staring at me, my hair curtaining my face; my ass, bare in the room's chill; the sting of my palm... and yet as I replayed it, again and again, a disturbed feeling began to spread through me.

Was it possible I had wanted my father to touch me so badly I would do anything?

Automatically, I reached for my phone and pulled it out of my pocket. I had forgotten I'd turned it off, and now I felt ill at the thought of confronting whatever had been deposited there. I wondered if my parents had tried to contact me, reproaching me for last night—or if Jojo had texted, to continue our discussion—or Sam, to remind me of my repulsive behavior—or Langham, changing his mind—

I would turn my phone on in twenty minutes.

Or an hour.

Down the sidewalk, a teenager was shouting into her phone, and I slowed to eavesdrop. She was wearing makeup and had already begun to highlight her hair; she was definitely taller than me. But as I neared it was clear she was distressed, and as she yelled into the phone she stomped her foot in helpless rage, making her look so young.

"You told Mom!" she screamed. Was she talking to her father? "You fucking idiot!" Her brother, probably. "I told you not to tell her! I told you it was a secret!"—and now her voice was breaking, she felt exposed and wronged. I hurried past; I didn't want to hear any more.

The burrito place was small and there were already two people in line. I squeezed in and waited to place my order, then sat at one of the tables to wait, looking out the dirty window onto the avenue. I watched a leaf twist through the air, silhouetted against the purpling sky. I felt mournful. A woman walked by with her pit bull, the leash stuffed into her pocket along with her hand. A breeze blew a piece of garbage into the dog's side and he jumped into a crouch, tail down. Something about this made me give a hollow laugh, but the woman bent down to soothe her dog, scratching the crown of his head, and I felt even more depressed. It wasn't just that I'd laughed at his fear; it was that no one cared to soothe me in that way.

How had my session with Freud begun? I remembered pulling his blanket up to my chest, Freud breathing steadily behind me... I had told him about the opera... his hands had been on my head—I had bit him!—me!—*I won your pain*—*you will obey me*—*I know what you want*, he had said, or had he?—

Stop! I threaded one hand through the hair at the nape of my neck, so that I could pull hard without anyone seeing. Hidden, my face betraying nothing, the comforting rush of pain. One of the men in line got his order and threaded his way out of the room, brushing against my elbow, so I dropped my arm and instead pressed my crotch into the hard plastic of my seat—*Why do you think you needed to do that?* But Freud hadn't been criticizing me, had he; wasn't it a gift that I had found a way to soothe myself?

The burrito was ready. I paid and went out to the street, sat on the curb to eat. It was a gift, maybe, but wasn't it an illness, too? What did it mean that I couldn't feel shitty for a minute without touching myself? What did it mean that I could come only when I was alone? Or— with Freud. It was the first time I had ever come in front of a man. Again I pictured myself draped over the arm of the couch, touching myself, smacking myself, my face contorted, probably, into something appalling—I chewed faster—I had come in front of him, I had told him about my father, how had I told him so much?—*you wanted your father to touch you so badly that you would do anything*—

A man walked by on the opposite side of the street, thick shoulders, meaty face. I couldn't see him clearly from this angle, but I was almost certain that he wore a mustache, walrus-like and heinous. Langham. *Thx for pretending nothing happened,* the fucking prick, Langham—

I swallowed a big bite, too quick, and "Fuck you!" I shouted across the street, a fleck of bean shooting out of my mouth. He didn't turn. "Fuck! You! You fucking prick! Langham! Fuck you!"

He still hadn't looked at me, so I stood, chucked the last few bites of the burrito in the trash, and brushed the dirt off my ass as I ran across the street.

"Hey! Langham! Hey! *Fuck you!*"

As I got closer, I began to have a sinking feeling, but I was on a conveyor belt, I couldn't stop, and then—*fuck you fuck you fuck you*—he turned around, and no, it wasn't him, it wasn't Langham at all.

What else had I imagined?

But the thought was too much to bear—I grabbed for my phone, and this time, I turned it on.

I wrapped my jacket tightly, as if to protect myself, as the screen gleamed to life in the center of my palm. My heart raced. I typed in my password.

Nothing.

I was stunned. Nothing?

What had I been hoping for?

And then, descending from the top of the screen, as if it had taken a moment to register, a voice mail from my mother, asking me to please call her back when I got the message.

I called back and her phone went to voice mail. Then I tried my father—voice mail, too. My ears started to ring, and I could have pretended it was worry—neither of them had picked up—but they often didn't answer, and besides it was Sunday afternoon, so they could easily be at a museum or the supermarket or otherwise occupying their time. And yet I had the sudden and sure knowledge that I needed to go back uptown. Not to check on them; not even, really, to discuss whatever it was my mother wanted to broach. It was something more troubling: it was I who needed to talk to them.

The ride uptown. The walk to their building, too-fit parents guiding their expensively clad children by the hands. *Hello, hello,* to the doorman, *how are you*—and then I was in the elevator, alone, staring at my reflection in the mirror, my wild hair, ascending to the twelfth floor.

The elevator doors opened. The garish carpet. The night before, my father standing in the doorway, taking me in, *That's very short*—I closed my eyes as I walked, the better to block out the deluge, trailing my fingertips along the walls as I always did, this time to guide me where I needed to go.

I rang the doorbell and waited a few beats, but no one came. This wasn't a shock; since they hadn't picked up their phones, I'd known they would probably be out. I would let myself in and wait for them inside.

I still had a key to their apartment, but it was in my dresser at home. I knew they kept a spare on top of the doorframe, a place so obvious it irritated me, yet out of some kind of schadenfreude I'd never told them that everyone knew to look there for the key. Who were they fooling? I had always half hoped, as a child, that a burglar would come while we were away, stealing all of my parents' psychology books, the copies of the magazines they'd been published in, their wedding album, everything that had nothing to do with me. I was terrified, though, that the burglar would come while we were home—terrified or desirous? I remembered lying awake at night, starting at every noise, wondering if this was the night he would come to kill us all; I had gory, fearful fantasies of finding my parents' bodies laid out on the kitchen floor... yet I wondered, now, if there was a wish embedded there, that they would be gone, that I would be free, that the "burglar," as I still thought of him, would see me, my sweet young face, my eyes big from pain, and would take mercy on me, would make me his.

The problem with the key was that I was too short to reach it. Once in a while I could jump, swipe the doorframe, and manage to knock it to the floor—yet this time, I was having no luck. I looked down the hallway; at the other end, a neighbor had left an umbrella out to dry. On the way, I passed the door to my parents' office and paused for a moment, pressing my fingers into the door. It was possible they were inside, doing research or writing, nonclinical work, yet it was unlikely on a Sunday. Anyway, if they were, I shouldn't disturb them, I should still wait for them in the apartment. Yet I felt rooted there, my fingers on the door, remembering all the times I'd stood at our peephole, peering down the hall, watching to see who came.

Like Olivia. Client Z. Back then, her hair had been long; I remembered watching from our door as it swished along her back like a metronome. I thought of the way she threw back her head to laugh once, at something my father had said when she opened the door. She had bared her throat to the light, and I could see through the peephole the ridges of her windpipe. Her mouth opened to the ceiling. Her neck so delicate, beckoning my father to place his lips there. The laugh had ended, and he had invited her into his office, and then he had closed the door. I had run to my room, slammed the door, sobbed, touched myself—

Had they been fucking each other?

I jerked my hand away from the door. Was it possible? I turned to lean my back against the wall, closing my eyes. Olivia. *What would that mean?* Freud would ask if he were here. *What would it mean, not to your parents, but to you?*

It would mean he could love, I would tell him. *That he could love, that he could touch—that he was hiding it from me, but that he could.*

He could, so if I tried hard enough, I could make him love me.

Once I'd grabbed the umbrella, I stood on tiptoes to swipe it across the top of the doorframe. With a soft thud, the key fell to the carpet. I put the umbrella back and let myself inside. I hadn't been in the apartment without my parents for... I couldn't remember how long. The place was eerie without them; I knew I'd spent many hours alone here as a child, and yet now that I didn't live here anymore, it was as though I'd snuck into a museum after hours. The lights were off, so the whole place was cast in the rich tones of the afternoon sun, streaming through the translucent curtains. I was nervous, closing the door behind me, not only because I was here in secret, but because once they returned, I didn't know what I would say. Only that I needed to say it.

I trailed my hand along the kitchen counters, which were sleek and spotless marble; surely the cleaning lady had recently wiped them down. There were no traces of the dinner party the night before. Inside the pantry were the familiar staples: no granola, no cereal, no bread; just lentils and almonds and chia seeds, lined up in glass canisters. There were three full spice drawers, which I always marveled at—to me, my mother's cooking, which she so prided herself on, was underflavored. My father was fooled; he thought she was the best cook in the world. Or did he? Was this his way of apologizing to her for his betrayal? It seemed unreal, and I tried to push the thought out of my head. *It's only salt,* I'd always wanted to say, or *Red pepper flakes won't kill you*; I had made a grand show, for a time, of dousing the dishes she made in salt and pepper after I'd taken a bite. Yet she'd replied only by grabbing the shakers out of my hand, worrying I would ruin the food, or maybe that I would eat so much salt I'd bloat up.

In the living room, I drew the curtains back and the sun poured in, making me squint. The Chrysler Building looked like a shadow of itself in the daylight; it was waiting for evening, when it could give everyone the finger. I walked past my parents' room, then changed my mind and entered. Inside my mother's walk-in closet, on top of the dresser, was a row of her perfumes. I made my way through the bottles, methodically removing each cap and drawing the dispenser to my nose. The scents weren't wildly different, each a variation on a theme that I found repellent, something like forest floor mixed with animal urine. I knew she loved this type of "woodsy" scent—the closest she felt comfortable getting to the outdoors. There was something irritating to me about not just the category of the smell, but the variations she had lined up, bottle by bottle—it seemed like a failure of character to me that she couldn't commit to one signature scent after all this time or, in opposition, that she hadn't collected wildly different scents as a form of play. I felt resentful, and also I felt sad.

Once I was finished, I made for my father's closet. The door was closed, and I paused, my palm pressed against it. Did I want to go inside? It had been a little more than a week, now, since my night here with Langham—the hairy round belly, my father's shoes. I didn't know that I was ready to revisit the space. Would doing so conjure such painful self-recrimination that I would lose my nerve to speak to them, just take myself home? And yet: Could I resist?

I opened the door and there it was: the closet, its immaculate rows of shoes and suits and shirts. Not a thing was askew. The carpet was beige; I could practically see the imprint of my back. Yet I felt a strange numbness. Had I wanted to feel nausea, revulsion, shame? There was the jacket I had tried on as a child—the one that had made my father laugh. I fingered the sleeve, then crouched down and ran my fingers along the backs of his shoes, and finally lay on my back in the middle of the closet, my father's belongings hanging around me, enfolding me. I could smell the faint odor of his shoes. I raised my knees into the position they'd been in, closed my eyes, conjured Langham's huffing face drawing closer and then farther away. I remembered again the man I'd accosted on the street, how he wasn't Langham at all. My stomach clenched and I screwed my eyes closed, drew my knees into my stomach and wrapped my arms around them. Did I want to masturbate? I figured I did. I almost always masturbated on my back, but now I flipped onto all fours, pulled my pants down to my knees, reached my hand between my legs, and bent my face toward the shoes, inhaling them, rubbing myself, faster, faster—the scent of feet and sweat—I closed my eyes and was in Pilz Bar again, draped over the couch—I shifted my weight so I could slap my ass with my free hand—Freud's eyes, the pulsation at his neck, the spire of the Chrysler Building, the twin cherries of a collarbone, the twin orbs of an ass...

By the time I heard my parents' key in the lock, I was in the living room, watching out the window as the sun inched toward the horizon.

"I'm here," I called out, so as not to startle them, but still my mother yelped. She came into the living room and I rose to embrace her. She hugged me to her and kissed my left eyelid—a joke between us that prompted the startling pinprick of tears. When I was little, she'd bent down to kiss me and had missed my cheek, getting me in the eye instead. It had made us laugh, and she'd started doing it on purpose every so often. She hadn't done it in so long I'd almost forgotten. It meant even more to me that she'd done it after last night, when I'd left early, when I'd been convinced she was livid—well, maybe she had been. I buried my head in her neck.

"What are you doing here?" she asked, pulling away as my dad walked in, shrugging off his jacket and draping it over the arm of the couch. "We didn't expect to see you."

"I got your voice mail," I said. "When I couldn't reach you, I decided to just come."

"Ah," my father said, pulling his phone out of his back pocket to see my missed call, then laying it on the side table. "We were at MoMA."

"Good?" I said. I wanted to hug him, even the awkward, pat-on-the-back kind, just to be near him, but it would require conspicuously crossing the several yards between us, then initiating the embrace—*Oh!* he might say, how awful—and I stopped myself.

He nodded: they'd seen a photography exhibit. My mother was more interested in abstract art, but I knew when she wanted to see that she took herself.

"So, why did you call?" I asked, and suddenly I became nervous. I hadn't thought this was why I'd come, but now I realized I was afraid to hear whatever it was they needed to say—a critique of my behavior last night, this month, this year? Or was it some dire piece of news? Had one of my grandmothers fallen ill? Were they giving up the practice, moving out of New York City; was there financial difficulty; were they splitting up?

"Come—let's sit down," my mother said. "Do you want anything to drink, eat?"

"I'm okay." I folded myself into the corner of the couch, and my father lowered himself into his arm-chair. My mother sat in the chair next to him, the two of them facing me. My father shifted forward, elbows on knees, then changed his mind and leaned back again. I realized I was sweating, my shirt damp and cold beneath my armpits. I took one of the decorative pillows onto my lap, pressing it into my stomach. Did they notice? *There's no need to be nervous,* I silently begged them to say. I pictured Freud putting his hands on my head, his fingertips on my eyebrows, and, for a brief moment, closed my eyes. Still, no one spoke; I wasn't sure if they were waiting for me to begin, but wasn't it my mother who had called me? The awkwardness was oppressive.

"Can you tell me what you called about?" I said. "You're making me nervous."

"Well, we aren't *making* you nervous," my father said. "Feelings aren't made by external circumstance. They're made by your own internal commands—" But I saw my mother cut him a look, and he stopped speaking short of where I knew he was going, that only I was responsible for how I felt. In a way, it was true. Yet it left me painfully, unbearably alone.

"We wanted to talk to you about last night," my mother said, and I raced to discover what she could mean before she said it—coming late, being drunk, leaving so abruptly—or had they found out about Langham?—finally. "We're concerned about you."

Did they mean I'd embarrassed them? Or that I had hurt their feelings? Was it about their colleagues, their friends? Was it about Langham after all?

My father cleared his throat. "Something seems a little... off with you," he said, and then echoed, "We're concerned."

"Where do I fit into your 'we'?" I said.

As soon as the words leaped from my mouth, I was ashamed. I felt more desperate than I had the night before, in my stiletto heels, begging everyone to look at me, notice me, love me—it was humiliating, my need, my deep and repulsive need.

"You are in our 'we,'" my mother said, but she was looking at my father, and I felt acutely separate from them.

"We want to help you," he said.

"You came very late and left very early," my mother said. "And"—she cleared her throat, she looked at the floor, here it was, it was coming—"you were very intox-icated."

So that was all. They really and truly did not know. I felt a swell of despair. Finally she looked back up and met my eyes.

"I'm sorry to embarrass you," I said. "I'm sorry you're ashamed of me."

"We aren't ashamed of you!" she said, but her pitch was unnaturally high, and I knew that, at least a little bit, they were.

"We're *concerned* about you," my father repeated. That "we." There were the two of them, and then there was me.

What was it, really, that had made them decide at *this* moment that I needed help? *She's unwell,* I imagined them saying—was that what I had been trying to convey to them my whole life? It occurred to me, not for the first time, how strange it must seem that my parents had never sent me to see someone. But it wasn't strange. To do so would have been to admit defeat; to have a child in therapy would have undermined everything they had tried to project. They did it themselves, with their rubber bands, their admonitions to "talk back" to my critical thoughts. I looked around the room: the fluffed pillows perched one in front of the other on the couch, like soldiers at attention; the satin coverlet, smooth and gleaming.

"But what made you think that now, of all times?" I said. This wasn't the first time I'd come late or left early, and it certainly wasn't the first time I'd been drunk. She had even offered me wine herself.

"Like I said, it was something about last night," my mother said, then looked to my father, but he didn't step in. "You seemed more... disconnected than usual." She was stroking the back of her left hand with her right pointer finger, her go-to nervous tic. I remembered myself on this very couch, Langham nearby, my distress enveloping me.

I thought back to all the times I'd felt that same suffocating cloud of despair. Was it right that they took no responsibility, that they acted as though I had arrived from another place entirely, another world? Wasn't it my father who had felt so overcome by... something, when I'd simply tried to hug him, that he'd smacked me?

"I'd like to talk about the time—about the time—" But I couldn't bring the words out of my throat. *You spanked me*, I thought. *Why did you spank me, when all I wanted was your love?* Would I ever really say this—could I dare? And what if I did? Did I think this would make him reconsider, did I think this would make him fold himself inside out for me, did I think he would let either of us see what was buried there? What would he say? *Yes, I spanked you. Everyone did it. Is that so bad?* Did I think he would ever tell me why he had become a psychologist, what he was trying to understand, or fix, or control? I couldn't imagine it, and this refusal was more than I could bear. This refusal; this incapacity. I thought back to the bar, to lying on the couch, and my yearning for Freud was so intense I could hardly stand it.

"About the time..." my father prompted, and I saw that his hands were tight around his knees. What did he fear I was going to say?

"About the time you spanked me," I said in a rush.

My words hung in the air.

"I don't remember that," he said finally.

I was stunned. He didn't remember. It was as though he had disowned me.

"It was after the opera," I said, "after *Werther*—"

But he only shook his head. "I don't remember ever doing that to you," he said.

In a panic, I searched his face for any sign that he knew what I was talking about. But I couldn't find one. It seemed that he genuinely could not recall, that the incident had vanished from his mind. Blinking rapidly, I looked toward my mother. "Mom," I said, but I realized she hadn't been there, and I had never told her a thing about it.

"I can't imagine your father would do that," she said, her words an abandonment. But I knew, I *knew*, I had not imagined this. And when I looked at my mother's hands I saw that her pointer finger had gained speed, it was stroking her other hand in a rapid circle.

"Have you ever cheated on Mom?" I blurted out, and as soon as I'd said it I was filled with regret.

"Why would you say that?" he said, and in truth I did not know. What had I hoped to accomplish, or provoke? Certainly not an admission—after what had just happened, that seemed impossible. Perhaps retribution. Or maybe, finally, I wanted to drive a wedge between them. To devastate their "we." As if I had that power. Again I thought about Olivia, her luscious windpipe. Was Olivia my way of convincing myself that I wasn't as left out as I'd always felt, that I wasn't quite as alone? Or was there something real there, some truth? I'd thought of my parents' bond as unbreakable, but had I ever seen them kiss? Had I seen them hold hands? I couldn't remember. I'd decided they were in love. *I* had decided that—me. They were a team, a pair, an exclusive club—but were they in love? Wasn't it odd that I'd never caught them fucking, or even suspected I'd walked in on something, not even once? Hadn't all my childhood classmates, at one time or another, caught their parents doing something they wished they could unsee? Were my parents just—what—colleagues? Was it simply a business arrangement? And what did that make me? *If my father could love Olivia, if he could love Client Z, that would mean he could love me...*

What else did you imagine was being withheld from you? Freud would say. *What else did you imagine your father was hiding?*

And what did I imagine? That he was having an affair?—or that he was gay?

The moment I thought it, I went rigid and cold. I saw his face warped into a grimace, the way he flinched when he was touched—*We can't know,* Freud would tell me, the most devastating truth of all. *We can't know.*

And did it matter? Did it matter, after all? There was repression, that I could know: repression of desire, repression that manifested in rage. Was my father closeted, or was he a repressed straight man? When I touched him, did he feel a desire that terrified him so much he was violent? To banish me, so he wouldn't have to deal with what I brought up in him?

It didn't matter. It was possible. It was all possible. The only known thing was that I craved more than he could give. And that since then, I'd internalized what he had done. I'd been banishing myself.

I thought of my childhood bedroom, just a few rooms away: the daisy-patterned wallpaper, the little bookshelf with the books I had escaped into as a child, the shelves that were still home to rows of stuffed animals. When I was young, after my mother had tucked me in at night, I would wish so hard for my father to come in afterward, say good night, tell me he loved me—wish so hard that I imagined he could read my mind. At times I whispered into the dark—*tuck me in, touch my hair, touch my cheek, tell me you love me*—and imagined the wisps of my words traveling through my bedroom and underneath the door and down the hallway and into the living room and right into my father's ears. *Why didn't he love me?* I wanted to ask Freud.

I think your father did love you, he would say. *I think he does love you. But it was not in the way that you needed. And perhaps this is the point: not why he couldn't connect with you, but that he couldn't connect with you. Perhaps the central acceptance you can make is that you will never fully know— never fully understand—your father. And he will never fully understand you.*

Was that possible—that I would never know why? That I wouldn't know for sure that my father had cheated on my mother, or that he was gay, or that he wanted me and this made him terrified? Why he parted his hair just so. Why he didn't like to be touched. *Sit* next *to Daddy.* Why he spanked me by the sink, or why he couldn't remember. Why he never came to tuck me in, why he didn't want me to put my head on his shoulder, let alone make a sandwich with his. I would only understand that he struggled—he wouldn't act this way if he didn't; he wouldn't have become a therapist, either. Neither of them would have. I would understand that, and that I couldn't get what I needed. It may have been what another child needed, but not me. And instead of shifting my need, my love, someplace else, I'd internalized it all. Of course I had. My parents had become a part of me. And I had been attacking them—the them inside of me: so I had been attacking myself. A painful solution, but one that meant I hadn't had to accept what they could not give me; I hadn't had to move on; I hadn't needed to let go.

But I want to let go, I would tell Freud if he were here.

Do you? he would say.

I did, but I didn't.

By taking flight into the ego, he would tell me, *love escapes extinction...*

Again I imagined his palms on the crown of my head.

Why didn't my father understand me? I would say.

This isn't about him understanding you, he would reply. *It's about you understanding you.*

My parents were still staring at me. I pressed the pillow deep into my stomach. Breath came in and out of my body slowly. I was a seashell, if you held your ear up to me you'd hear the ocean.

"I'm sorry," I said to my father. "I shouldn't have said that."

"Of course I've never cheated on your mother," he said.

I looked at my mom, who had always been a mystery to me, her mind so very far away. She blinked rapidly, as though trying not to cry, or maybe it was because she could only stand to look at me for those few moments in between each blink, each reprieve.

"Mom, I'm so sorry," I said.

"We only want to help you," she said, looking shrunken and wounded to me.

They wanted to help me, and I did need help. More than that, I wanted it. But I thought of their rubber bands, their thought tracking, their flow charts—the help I needed wasn't the kind they could give.

What I needed was Freud.

"Thank you for that," I said. "Sincerely. I'm going to think about it and—can we talk about it more later?"

"We would really feel more comfortable if we figured something out now," my mother said, but I stood.

"Could you please—just sit back down and we'll talk it through—"

"I promise to think about it," I said, nodding as though it were final.

She nodded in reply, taking a deep breath. "Okay," she said, then stood to hug me. My father pressed his hands to his knees as if to stand as well, but—

"It's okay," I said, and meant it. I put my palm up in farewell. "I'll talk to you soon. I'll let myself out."

At the door, I stopped: the key. I could go back into the living room and give it to my parents; the thought repelled me. I could toss it, over and over, until finally it landed on the doorframe. Or I could leave it on the floor, as if some minor earthquake had taken place. (Hadn't it?) Instead I went to the kitchen and left it in the middle of the counter for my parents to find. A reminder: *I was here.* And then I left, twisting the doorknob lock and closing the door.

Chapter 8

It was a long journey, and I was grateful. I needed my mind to stop pulsing with the exchange I'd just had; I needed all my reserves for the encounter to come. I took the 6 to Union Square to transfer to the R. I prayed, as I walked, that the platform would be free of performers. It wasn't impossible; it was a Sunday evening. But I heard him as I walked down the stairs—not the young violinist, the better option if there had to be one, but the elderly man playing the saw.

Oh, how I loathed the saw. I wanted to clamp my hands over my ears. He pulled his bow across the instrument, releasing a high-pitched wailing, the most mournful sound I'd ever heard. This was my cue to turn around, to run far away, but my legs were taking me down the stairs, and then there was the train roaring into the station, overwhelming the sound of the saw, and then it screeched to a halt. The doors opened, and I was on my way back to Freud.

Outside the bar, I stood by the window, peering through the slats. I saw Ed pouring beers for a young couple. They seemed to either have just met or be on a first date—whatever it was, it was going well. They couldn't stop grinning and bashfully looking at each other and then away again. He leaned down to whisper something to her, and I saw her swallow hard at the feeling of his breath on her ear. In another mood it would have made me nauseated and enraged, but at this moment I felt magnanimous, even hopeful. *Go ahead,* I thought, *have your love. I have Freud.*

Until I saw him. Farther down the bar, a second bartender: bearded. Deep and piercing eyes.

But not Freud.

I felt as though I might faint. I managed to get myself inside and stood at the bar, waiting to speak to him. Ed saw me first.

"Hey, you!" he said. "The usual?"

"No," I said. "I, um..." I didn't know how to say it. "That guy," I said finally, and pointed to him. "Is he new?"

"Yup," said Ed, "started just this past week. Good guy."

Dizzy. *Need a couch.* I told Ed I had to use the bathroom.

"Have at it," he said, but I waited until he turned away and, instead of heading for the bathroom, slipped off to the thin hallway.

It was dank. There was a mop in a bucket, the handle leaning against the wall, the water clouded black. I hadn't noticed that before. There, at the end of the hallway, was the closed door. Freud's door.

My palms were slick. Was it Freud's office, just as I remembered—or a storage closet, full of cleaning supplies? I drew nearer, just as I had earlier, three feet away, now two...

And then I stopped. I couldn't do it. I didn't want to know.

I sank to the floor, my back against the wall. I strained my ears, but I could hear nothing behind the door. That didn't mean anything, did it? He could still be there, reading, writing—or he could not be there at all. What if I had imagined everything? What was wrong with me? Was there any chance Freud was real? I wanted desperately for him to be—and did this mean I was sick, or did it simply mean that I could give myself what I needed? *If you eat me up, there will be nothing left.* And yet hadn't I eaten him up—wasn't he, at this very moment, inside me? I closed my eyes. I expected to feel extraordinarily alone, but instead I felt the least alone I had ever known.

By the time I got up to make my way home, night had fallen. Ed was still at the bar. His eyes flicked up at me, and a strange look passed over his face. *What is wrong with me?* At once I felt repulsed by him, by his shtick and everything about him, and I was shocked I had ever responded to him with anything like pleasure.

"Good night," I said, walking past him toward the door.

"Hey, you okay?" he called, but I ignored him.

I walked home, pulling my jacket tight around me. There was a missing dog sign plastered to a lamppost, four photos of a little Havanese named Henrietta: "She is an emotional/hearing service dog to a little nine-year-old girl... Not just a dog, she's family... a loving home with a backyard she loves to run around in... Please, if you see her... please..."

I shoved my hands into my pockets. There was the napkin. I couldn't look at it. What if it said nothing, what if it was just an empty scrap? I rubbed it hard between my fingers, then closed my fist around it, pressing it into my palm.

The street looked desolate. I dreaded seeing Jojo. I remembered her sitting on the stairs, her phone in her hand. She'd brought up Sam and had held out her arm, which, at the party, I'd squeezed in rage. I tried my best to recall how our conversation had ended; had she said something about moving out? Or had I? I had run outside and vomited over the railing, I recalled in a blurry snapshot, and then I had said something that had made her cringe.

I found Jojo in the kitchen, making her nighttime tea, grating ginger into a pot of water set to boil. I knew she would pour the concoction over a huge strainer and into a mug, squeeze in a lemon slice, stir in a spoonful of raw honey. She hadn't heard me come in, and I stood in the living room, watching her. *Say something.* My pulse was in my ears. She stirred the pot, the steam wafting toward her face. *Just say hello.* But I couldn't make the words come out. She tapped the wooden spoon against the side of the pot and laid it in the ceramic spoon rest and turned toward the fridge for her lemon. She saw me and jumped.

"Oh my God." She put her hand on her chest, breathing heavily. *"Fuck."*

"Sorry," I said. "I was going to say something, I just—I couldn't—"

But she had started to laugh with relief, a laugh that soon blossomed into hysterics, uncontrollable.

"Are you... ?" I said, and I had meant to say *okay*, but then I was laughing, too, slowly at first, then doubled over. "Hi, I'm home," I said in between spasms, the joke being that it had come at least two minutes too late; as soon as I said it I realized it wasn't funny and braced myself for the laughter to end, but she liked it, she liked my joke, and we were off again, gasping for breath.

Afterward, we sat on the couch, two cups of tea in hand—she'd made me one, too. But the mood had shifted; after the mania of our howling, I felt self-conscious again and then, remembering our last conversation, afraid. One spate of laughter couldn't undo what I had done— digging my nails into her arm, fucking her brother, puking into the bushes. I pressed both palms to the hot mug, palms burning almost too much, then sipped it, feeling the tartness at my jaw.

"How was your day?" I asked tentatively.

"Good." She nodded, holding my gaze. I waited for her to say more, but she didn't, as though she didn't want to let me in at all, even to the minutiae of her Sunday. Was it because she was figuring out how to broach yesterday's conversation again, or because she really didn't want to be my roommate anymore? I studied her face for signs but found it unreadable, and took another sip of tea, breaking our eye contact.

"I spent the day with Sam," she said with an exhale. "I wasn't sure if I should mention it. But yeah—we hung out in the park."

I chewed on my thumbnail, unable to look at her, then realized I must look like a child sucking her thumb and took it out again.

"How is he?" I said.

"He's totally fine," she said. "We honestly didn't even talk about it."

This should have been good news, but I felt forlorn.

"Well—good," I said. "Look, I'm really sorry, again."

"It's really okay," she said. "I was heated up about it last night—I get protective around my siblings, you know? But he's a man, he can handle himself." At the word "man," my throat tightened. Jojo smiled a little, sadly, I thought. "We don't have to talk about it anymore." Her tone was final, and rather than feeling relieved, I felt very much alone.

"So you *don't* want me to move out, is what you're saying?" Even as I formed the words, I knew they were senseless. *Why do you need me to betray you?* But I needed her to tell me that she wanted me here, I needed it desperately.

"You don't really think that, do you?" she said. "Like, seriously?" She shook her head, almost rolling her eyes, and in her reaction I was reminded of how I'd felt with intractable students who seemed to willfully misinterpret my directives. The one who'd left her book closed on her desk when I asked them to turn to a particular page, then sat twisting her hair round and round her finger, looking straight at me, as if daring me to challenge her; or the one who—moments after I'd said, *Good morning, let's get started*—had rapped on the window next to his desk to get the attention of his friend, then made a series of gestures I couldn't possibly understand.

"No," I admitted. "I don't really think that." I paused, then added softly: "I just wanted to hear you say it."

"I want you to live here," she said, and put her hand on my knee. "Really. And not just because I'd be fucked without your rent."

"Why, then?" I said. I knew I was probing so forcefully I'd repulse her, but I couldn't stop myself. I needed to know—or I needed to ruin the whole thing, have it be over, have it again be controlled by me.

She let out a puff of laughter. "Okay, fine," she said. "I'll bite. You're neat." She ticked off a finger. "You do pay the rent on time. And, maybe most importantly, I like your stories."

"I'm a disaster," I said.

"Maybe." She shrugged but smiled, so I knew it was a joke. "But you're not a *monster*."

I had assumed either she had bought my polished faux self—impenetrable and cool, firmly in control of my feelings—or that she had detected, underneath this projection, the disgusting and dangerous person I knew myself to be. But perhaps all she saw was someone vulnerable and sad. A mess. Not a danger.

I had an almost unbearable urge to tell her about Freud. Was it because I was desperate to ruin the relationship, to finally push her over the edge? Nothing I had done so far had been enough; maybe this last thing would make her see who I really was. Or—and this was not impossible—was it because I had never had a real friend before? I wasn't sure if this counted, but it was as close as I'd come. I sipped the tea again; it felt like literal proof of kinship. And somehow her beauty felt protective; it would shield us from anything bad that would happen if I told. She had both hands curled around her mug and was bent toward it, taking a sip, her hair hanging around her face like a cozy tent; but she was looking at me over the rim of the mug, as if trying to figure out what I was going to say.

"Can I tell you a secret?" I said.

She sat up straight and brought the mug down toward her knees, shook her hair out of her face. "Hit me."

"I thought I saw Freud," I said quickly, before I could change my mind.

She leaned toward me, squinting.

"Sigmund Freud," I said.

"You thought you saw him."

I nodded.

"On the street?"

"No," I said. "In a bar."

"As in, you saw someone who looked like him?"

"I don't know," I said. "He was so real..."

Jojo stared at me, eyes wide, but she didn't look away. "Keep going," she said, her voice soft.

"He was at Celeste's party, too," I said. "I mean, I saw the back of his head."

"At Celeste's party."

"Yes." I looked down at her long, slender feet. I wanted to hold them. As if to her toes, her kind and delicate toes, I whispered, "Did you see him there?"

"Hmm," she said, and when I dared to glance back at her she flashed a quick, awkward smile. "The guy with the beard? Her painter friend?"

I shook my head. It was him. It had to be.

"I told him about my life," I said. "Not at the party. After."

She nodded.

"I lay on my back on a couch," I said. "And"—how far would I go?—"he did a laying of hands." Then I stopped.

Now she did look afraid. I wanted to suck the words back out of the air. Why had I told? My precious secret, or was it my shame? But I was scared, too, and it comforted me, feeling it together.

"I'm not sure I know what to do with that," she said, and swallowed. "Do you think, maybe..." She paused.

I looked straight into her eyes, to let her know it was okay.

"Maybe you should see someone?" She scrunched up her face.

I pursed my lips. I felt empty.

"It isn't a punishment," she said.

"I know," I said. But I didn't know where to turn. If it wasn't my parents, if it wasn't Freud, if it wasn't her, I was stuck, I was trapped and alone.

"Thanks for listening," I said. "I'm going to figure that out." I faked a yawn. "I'm going to go to bed."

"Hey, are you sure?"

"Yeah. I'm exhausted." I was desperate to leave.

"If you need help with it, I'm here," she said, and I nodded and stood and left the room.

Up in my bedroom, I lay with my computer propped up against my knees and opened up a browser window. I stared at the cursor, blinking in the search bar. *Maybe you should see someone...* I was so tired. Maybe I should just see a therapist like my parents—one of their colleagues, even.

It had worked for Olivia, hadn't it? Based on our conversation, they might even help me pay for it—but the thought of this made me want to throw my laptop across the room. Instead, without even thinking, I typed "Freud laying of hands."

It was ridiculous. But I moved through the search results as if possessed, page after page. There was his face, his penetrating gaze. I touched my fingertip to the screen. *Hi.* Yes, that was him. Not the painter. Freud. And another page, and another—and, finally, there it was. Freud hadn't come to his technique recommendations immediately. Of course he hadn't. In the beginning, when he was inventing a discipline from whole cloth, he had tried everything. He had tried hypnosis. And—yes, I bit my fingernail to keep myself from crying out with relief—he had tried something called the "pressure technique." In order to unearth repressed memories, Freud would place his hands on patients' heads and press down, calling to their unconscious through his touch.

He was across the table from me, his eyes boring into mine.

I said, "Can I hold your hand?"

His hands were folded before him, and now he unfolded them: a blooming. He moved his open palms toward me and I slipped my fingers inside. With my thumbs I stroked his fingers, one by one. His eyes still bore into mine.

"Can I touch your arms?"

He stretched them across the table and I traced my fingernails along the soft skin, underneath the cuffs of his jacket, then over his sleeves, all the way up to the creases inside his elbows. His eyelids became heavy, but still, he looked into my eyes.

We were standing now. "Can I hug you?" I said, and then our bodies were fused into one. My cheek lay on his chest. He ran his palms along my shoulders, my arms, down and then up again, memorizing me; then he drew me to him again, pressing me close. I could feel his heartbeat against my ear. I clutched his jacket in my fists. My breath was quick against him. I looked up.

"Can I..."

And then his lips were on mine. He kissed in my favorite way, dragging his teeth lightly over my bottom lip, then letting me do the same. I took his face in my hands, then his head, laced my fingers through his hair; he let out a tiny gasp only I could hear. *More,* I thought or maybe said, *more, more, I want more and even more —*

A clatter awoke me. My laptop had slid to the floor. The fog was dissipating; I blinked through it, reached down to grab the computer. Miraculously, it was still intact, just dented at one corner. I must have fallen asleep with it still on top of me. The lights were on, but it was pitch black through the window, which meant I hadn't overslept. I moved my gaze to the radiator, its interlocking little portals; the dresser; the mirror. Yesterday came back in threads: going straight to Freud; the couch; biting his finger—*I won your pain*—the opera—coming in front of him—*fuck*—the pulse in his neck—accosting a stranger on the street—what was real? I had gone to my parents'— here my stomach began to turn—*Have you ever cheated on Mom?*—my mother's finger, moving in a frantic circle—*I don't remember ever doing that to you —*

Hand between my legs. *Can I...* my hand tracing Freud's arm—his soft lips, his teeth, his hair in my hands—two orbs of an ass—a stingray, a laugh—my back against a fence—a button, pressing into me—my hair, yanked back—eyes boring into me—

It took no time at all, and I was back to myself.

I had half an hour before I officially had to wake up, so I opened the laptop. The tabs I'd pulled up the night before were still open, and there he was: his intimate glare. "*Good morning*," I whispered to the screen, and then my eye flicked to the next open tab, the "pressure technique." My crotch was still pulsing and I pressed my fingertips into it, not trying to come now but calming myself. *My vagina is sick*—these words from childhood floated through my mind and I gave a little laugh, pressed more firmly, as if to tell my vagina that it was safe, it was okay, it could calm down now and spring back to life another time. The pressure technique, all right.

And yet I was still wet, I couldn't calm down, I needed to masturbate again right away. I missed Freud, I missed him so deeply it hurt my whole body. "*Freud,*" I whispered— if he was a part of me, couldn't I call him to me? But nothing happened. "*Freud,*" I tried again, "*can you come back? Please? Come here and just talk to me, I promise not to touch you, I promise not to touch myself, I'll just lie here and talk, just please come back...*"

And yet he didn't. I felt like sobbing, and instead punched my fist into the bed, then spun onto all fours and began pounding my pillow, hooks and jabs into the silence. *Fuck you, Freud, fuck you for leaving me! Fuck you!* And then, finally, I could just cry.

What if I could never get him back? Was I destined—doomed—to be forever alone?

Only the day before, I had sat outside his office, unable to reenter. Was he real? Did it matter? I didn't want to know; I couldn't know. Not yet. But something else was increasingly and inescapably clear: something had happened that I could not control, something I could not even understand.

Despondent, I pulled the computer back onto my lap. There was his face, so like the one I knew. *My Freud.* What did I have left? Only this image of him? Then I wanted a million of them: I would plaster his face all over my walls. I would find every photo of him—I typed "Freud" into the search bar, then pulled up his face in tab after tab after tab, touching myself underneath the computer, its flat surface hot against the back of my hand—

See someone.

The words arrived as I came, not from my parents, not from Jojo, but from me.

See someone. As in: you are not the only human being on this planet. As in: you are not alone.

If I couldn't have Freud, if I couldn't have him *right now*, then I wanted as close as I could get. I knew this was impossible. My parents had said as much: *No one believes his ideas anymore.*

But didn't they? I wondered. Didn't someone believe it? Didn't I?

Next to the tabs upon tabs of Freud's face, I pulled up a new one: "psychoanalysis nyc."

And there they were—pages and pages of them, on and on, more psychoanalysts than I could have dreamed up. I was overwhelmed, whether by the number of them or the relief of knowing they were out there, waiting for me, I didn't know. The screen swam before me; I closed my eyes and clicked at random. The page that opened had no photograph, just a name and a short paragraph. "Successful therapy depends on the patient and the analyst working together to understand the roots of the patient's pain..."

Together.

It was still pitch black out, but the number listed was an office phone, so I knew it wouldn't wake her up. I reached for my phone, on the floor next to my bed, and dialed the number. I was shivering, though my room was warm, the radiator blasting despite what was only a fall chill. Her voice mail picked up. I hung up, heart racing. I laid the phone on my stomach, masturbated again—just one more time—or, well, who was I kidding—then wiped my hand on my sheets and called her again. This time, I left a voice mail. I wanted to set up a consultation as soon as possible.

Jojo had left my three good shirts hanging on my door-knob; she did this from time to time when I fell asleep before choosing my work outfit, so that I wouldn't wake her up in the morning. My favorite of the three was a sleeveless white silk button-down with a pointed collar, which I would wear underneath a black sweater. I liked buttoning the shirt all the way up to my neck, liked the way the little sweater hugged me, how I looked like both a girl and a boy. I would wear this with my fitted trousers, to heighten the androgyny; I was powerful in this outfit, playing a role that wasn't quite me. But that was teaching, too: I was the best version of myself. The trousers should have been hung up, but I felt I could ask Jojo for only so much closet space, so these I wore more often than was really appropriate, to reduce their tendency to wrinkle. I wondered if my students noticed; it was only a month in, but I'd worn these pants at least twice a week. Now I shook them out, then put them on my bed to smooth over the creases.

I would be good today.

I hoped intensely that she would call me back.

Chapter 9

The subway ride to school was the same as to my parents';
I wondered every day whether I would run into them on
the street and prayed I wouldn't. I hadn't yet; the route
didn't require me to pass by their apartment—they were
west of the subway, on Park Avenue, while the school was
a couple of avenues east—and, if I thought about it for
a minute, it made no sense that I would see them. They
worked from home and avoided going east if they could
help it. Did I think they would go to the bodega for a
soda? Really? But a part of me also liked that they were
nearby—that I could go hide out in childhood whenever I
wanted, theoretically. Or maybe it was the exact opposite:
that I was deliberately snubbing them every day, assert-
ing my power.

"Morning, Lillian," I said to the secretary at the front
desk, whom I'd known since I'd gone to this school myself.
I always wondered if the students thought I was pathetic
for returning to teach here; I'd thought that of one of my
own teachers, Ms. Chester. It *was* pathetic, in a way. And
yet Ms. Chester was old, or at least had seemed so to me
then—she must have been in her late thirties at the time.
She'd since moved on to a different school. I figured I had
a few years here before my expiration date.

I liked myself here, far better than I liked myself anywhere else. I hadn't as a student; I'd felt alienated even
before I'd started to make a mess by fucking around, but
teaching here was like getting a second chance, starting

fresh. I was a good teacher, in between the impatient bursts that overtook me from time to time, like the one on Friday. My knuckles on the desk; her frightened young face. I would have to repent for that. I would, at the very least, apologize. But when things were going my way, I was good at teaching, I was quite good, and I really did know this. I did care about something.

I took the long way around the corridor to my classroom—to the right, along three legs of the square that was this building, instead of to the left. Students were slamming their locker doors closed, jogging to class with their backpacks thumping against their sides. I took this route to avoid a certain teacher I'd fucked the first week of school, drunk at happy hour; we had run into each other a handful of times since, despite my maneuverings, and nothing terrible had happened besides my upswell of shame and disgust. Yet I wanted to minimize contact as much as I could. He was the only staff member I'd slept with, and I was determined to keep it that way—even if the other teachers found out, that could be seen as normal, I knew, sleeping with a coworker. *One* coworker. Beyond that was dangerous terrain. Beyond that they'd see me, really. For now, they saw *this* me: teacher-me. Trousers-me. I was competent here, I could do my job, even if I didn't deserve the fellowship I'd gotten to do it. I thought of the papers I'd promised to hand back today, still sitting in their accordion folder. My students would ask about them, I knew—Friday, I would promise. I could do that much.

Today I was starting to teach William Styron's *Darkness Visible*. One benefit of teaching high school English was that, unlike teaching elementary school, say, I needed only one lesson plan per day, which I'd do over and over. Of course, in the drama of the weekend, I hadn't even made a lesson plan, but I knew I could wing it; this book, one of the first open accounts of depression, was one I'd read at least seven times. I had marked up my copy heavily; each page was a landscape of underlines, check marks, exclamation points in the margins. The account was dire and raw, not necessarily approved material for a high school, and definitely not on any of the tests the students would have to take at the end of the year. But to me it was clear that many of them—high achievers, for the most part—were struggling, and that Styron's plain description of what it was like to be engulfed in this way might help them feel less alone. It had done so for me, at least for the moments I was absorbed in it, even if the feeling didn't last far beyond when I closed the cover. It wouldn't fix them; fixing wasn't a book's job. But it might be their friend.

"Talk to me about this opening sentence," I said in first period, after I'd apologized about the papers. I had expected them to be upset, but they were mostly still half asleep. Only a couple of students shifted anxiously in their seats, fiddled with their pens. "'In Paris on a chilly evening late in October of 1985 I first became fully aware that the struggle with the disorder in my mind—a struggle which had engaged me for several months—might have a fatal outcome.' What is he doing here?"

I looked from student to student; some of their uniforms were wrinkled like pajamas. I remembered wearing that exact uniform, sitting in those very seats, not so long ago. In the classroom, as a student, I could forget about the me that existed everywhere else—the person I was to my parents, the person I was pressed up against the bathroom stall door with a boy's finger inside me. Once the bell rang and I was sitting facing the teacher, looking no one my age in the eye, I could relax. But only then. Maybe nothing had changed.

After a moment my favorite student—Moira, a skinny girl with a sharp, smart chin who nodded avidly at everything I said—shot up her hand.

"He uses the word 'fatal,'" she says. "That's a big deal."

"Why?" I said.

"Well, we know it wasn't actually fatal; otherwise, how would we be reading it? But it's still..." She moved her head in tiny circles, a gesture I had come to know well, as she searched for the words. "We know it was close. And so it raises a million questions."

"Which is why I *could. Not. Put. It. Down*," said Adrien, my other favorite, thrusting the book into the air on each word, her glorious halo of hair—tips dyed a bleached blond—shimmering as she moved. "It sets up the stakes."

"Yes," I said, trying not to show how thrilled I was that they'd related to it as I had. We'd been talking about stakes for the past couple of weeks, about the different ways in which literature can demand our attention. "The stakes. Exactly. And then—can someone read the rest of the opening paragraph?" The rest were coming out of their sluggish haze, but slowly. I scanned the class; most of them stared at their desks to avoid catching my eye—I silently begged someone to volunteer, I hated cold-calling, it made me anxious— and then there it was, brilliant Moira's hand in the air.

As she read, I remembered a conversation with one of the other teachers, an aggressive middle-aged man, who had challenged my choice to teach this particular book when I'd told him at happy hour. "It's about suicide," he'd said, looking incredulous. "Aren't you worried that it'll be contagious? Do you seriously want blood on your hands?"

"That's absurd," I'd told him. "It doesn't work that way. You can't induce despair by writing about it! No one ever committed suicide because of a book!"

Still, in the days since that conversation, I'd worried. If I hadn't been so preoccupied, I probably would have chosen to teach something else. And yet now, seeing the students' reactions—after Moira finished reading, we began to talk of Styron's prose, the relentless accretion of black-and-white language, "gloom," "dread," "alienation," and how it so incandescently captured what it was like to be submerged in depression, in "melancholia"—I knew there was nothing at all to what this teacher had said.

After half an hour, I broke them into groups and assigned each a task: you discuss the narrative persona Styron employed to do this work; you discuss why he might have chosen not to disclose his childhood trauma until the end of the book; you discuss the way he grapples with whether language is adequate to the task he is asking it to accomplish. As they turned to one another and their adolescent din filled the room, I remembered how excruciating I had found this type of group work as a student, how I'd wanted to work on my own or to sit listening to my teacher. Was it just that I wanted control? Or was it the intimacy of group work—being obliged to respond, being looked at—that so distressed me? Sitting in the classroom, I could be invisible;

even when my teacher and I locked eyes, there was the protection of that roomful of other students. I had known then that I wanted to teach, to get to come to a classroom every day forever. One of my students covertly reached into his backpack to check his phone, and I remembered my message to the analyst and felt a swell of anxiety and grabbed for my phone, too.

But there was nothing. She hadn't called.

Nor had she by third period. That was also the class in which I had the student I'd spoken to sharply on Friday, Lacey. For fifty-five minutes, I averted my eyes; she was blatantly texting, and though technology was prohibited throughout the school, I pretended I didn't notice. I was reminded of Langham, passing his gaze over me so easily, then the encounter on the street—*fuck you*—and dove with increased fervor into the text, close-reading a paragraph line by line, until the train of thoughts abated. Could I get away with not talking to her one-on-one? It wasn't like she had skipped school; obviously she was *acting out* with her texting, but not so disruptively that I couldn't just ignore it for the rest of the year. But what if she never recovered? What if she texted the entire year long, disrupting class— what if the rest of the students followed suit? She probably talked to the other students about me behind my back. They probably had a lot to say about how often I'd worn these pants.

After class, I called Lacey over. As she approached, I put great attention into arranging the papers on my desk, avoiding looking at her until the last possible second.

She stood a few feet away from me, hip jutting out, backpack slung over one shoulder—distant, defiant, like the popular girls I'd gone to school with here. I was scared of her. But then I remembered the teenage girl talking on the phone on the street, how vulnerable she was under all that bravado, how young.

"I want to apologize for the way I spoke to you on Friday," I said.

"It's fine," she said, giving me a tight smile.

"It was my own impatience," I continued, to convince her I was really and truly sorry and to win her admiration back, if she'd ever had any. I had the urge to prostrate myself before her and beg her to forgive me. "It wasn't appropriate. I'm truly, truly sorry."

"It's fine," she repeated, and again gave me that tight smile. *Forgive me!* And yet there was something in her taut expression that called to mind my mother's the day before. She was judging me. She didn't respect me—she didn't even like me. I felt the desire to grab her—the same surge of emotion that had overcome me on Friday, when I'd spoken to her so sharply; the same surge that had compelled me to dig my fingernails into Jojo's arm, that had made me shove Freud backward outside the bar—and made a fist, digging my nails into my own palm instead.

"Thank you," I said, my heart pounding, "I appreciate that," and turned away before I could do anything, grabbing an eraser and furiously wiping at the board. "See you tomorrow," I called without turning around, my words bouncing off the chalkboard and back toward me.

I had made it.

And then, at lunch, there it was. She was booked all day, but could squeeze me in at four o'clock. School ended at three, which meant I had an hour to kill before my consultation. Sixty minutes for anxiety to pickle my insides. Was I really going to do this—really going to go see a psychoanalyst? And what was I planning to say? I had no idea. I should cancel. I took my phone out of my pocket, prepared to dial her number—and yet I didn't even put in my passcode. I didn't want to cancel the appointment. I just wanted it to be now. I didn't want to have to think, I didn't want to have to wait, I never wanted to wait, I wanted everything the second I thought it, I wanted to inhale the whole world.

3:05. I had put all my papers in my bag; I had tidied my desk. Fifty-five minutes to kill. She was across the park, on Riverside Drive, which meant I could spend a good half hour walking across town. Twenty-five minutes to kill, then. I would walk very slowly. *To kill*. It was a vicious expression, *killing time*, as if none of us really wanted to be alive at all.

And yet didn't I? Would I have made the appointment if I didn't? Didn't I want to be alive so badly I was about to burst?

I walked through the building the long way, as I had coming in. The teacher I'd fucked was not in sight, thank God. But standing in the entry to the building, talking to her hanger-on friend, was Lacey. My chest tightened. She had long, straight, shiny hair, the kind I'd always envied, and as I inched toward her she flicked it over her shoulder, giving her "friend" a smug little laugh. The other girl looked up at her, starved for more. Lacey glanced around and caught me coming toward them, then gave me that taut smile again.

"See you tomorrow," she said, but there was something hard in her eyes.

I ran my tongue back and forth along the roof of my mouth—*it's a dick*—but dicks weren't the only thing I loved; I loved teaching, I did love my students, I did love Freud.

"Yes," I said, "see you tomorrow," and I brushed past them and out into the windy autumn afternoon, hair whipping into my mouth and all around my face.

I walked across the park and all the way to the other side of the island, then the fifteen blocks up West End. At the building on the corner, the doorman appeared to know every canine in the neighborhood; he squatted and threw open his arms, and they pranced over, tails swinging. "Ziggy!" he shouted. "Socks!" "Bernadette, my girl!" Two women in pencil skirts and a man in paint-covered pants and boots waited in line at the coffee cart. A mother with a heavy Russian accent spoke sharply to her unfazed daughter: "It like you don't know even where you *live*!"

The building faced Riverside Park. I was still early, so I crossed over and sat on a bench. Nearby, a dark-bearded dad in rolled-up khakis and boat shoes, bare ankles catching the breeze, watched his two girls run in a circle, round and round, trailing streamers behind them. One of them saw me and gave a coy smile, so unanticipated it made me remember about laughter. The dad was relaxed, tilting his face up into a beam of sun, even as the wind blew his hair back like stalks of grass, and so his girls were relaxed, too, safe and elated.

One of the girls tripped and caught herself with her palms on the concrete. There was a pause while she registered the pain, and I braced myself for her cry. But her dad was walking over to her, not frantically, but with purpose; he was squatting next to her, putting his hand on her back. "You're okay," he told her, rubbing her small back: not a question, a statement. Not panic, a safety blanket. She was okay. She nodded, pushed herself back onto her feet, brushed off her knees. He gave her a gentle push and she was off running again.

It was time. I was nervous. I crossed back over, I entered the building, my palms were clammy, I told the doorman I was looking for 3C.

"Yes, miss, you have an appointment?"

"Yes."

He picked up the phone—"Young lady here to see you" —then nodded at me. "The elevator to the right, miss."

In the elevator, I put my hands in my pockets, pulling my jacket taut around the back of my neck. I felt myself shivering from fear or excitement and clenched my jaw to steady it. I was fiddling with something in my pocket, and when I registered what I was doing, I nearly laughed from surprise. The napkin.

It was still there. Which meant—what? Did it mean he was real? I could take it out and see: Were the words he'd written etched there, or weren't they? And what if they weren't? Would I ever accept this? There was no way. Either they were there or they had been rubbed off by my hands.

Yet I couldn't stop thinking about it. *Come back.* If they weren't there, I would be devastated. Would I ever recover? I wasn't sure that I would. But if I didn't look now, the torment wouldn't cease; I would wonder, every second until I looked, what I would find.

The elevator opened. There was still time: five minutes. Outside her office, I screwed my eyes closed. I took the napkin out of my pocket and felt for the corner, ripping off a tiny piece, then put it in my mouth, letting it disintegrate. *I'm here.* The next bit I chewed and swallowed. The next bit I rolled around my teeth, letting it massage my gums. The next bit went down like a vitamin. And then the next, and the next, and the next. *If you eat me up, there will be nothing left.* And yet I had found a way. He was still here. He was inside me, he was part of me, I would never let go, or perhaps I had, perhaps this was my only way of releasing him.

I went inside. There was a small waiting room with two offices abutting it. It looked a bit like my parents' own office waiting room: a couch, a few chairs, an end table with fanned-out magazines, a watercooler.

Just as I sank into one of the hard-backed chairs, scanning the selection of highbrow magazines on the end table, her door opened. "Come in," said her floating head.

In her office, we sat across from each other in silence. She was close to what I'd pictured, but the differences were stark enough to notice. Her hair, dark brown—expected—I'd imagined cut into a blunt bob, but it was long and thick, and she wore it gathered into a bun at the nape of her neck. I wondered if I would ever see it untied, hanging loose over her shoulders. I imagined I had a lot of time. I had pictured her more matronly, but she was only around forty and slight. Her eyes, which were unremarkable in my imaginings, were in reality a startling blue green.

Her gaze didn't leave my face, but it was soft, and I felt comfortable in it. The silence was warm and soothing and slow, like we were lounging in a bath together. I almost laughed at my bizarre association, but I knew she would ask me what I was laughing about, so instead I kept quiet, giving myself a few more moments to look around the office.

It had a certain resemblance to Freud's. Though she sat across from me, there was a chair positioned behind the couch on which I sat, so that when I began to lie down for sessions, as I assumed I soon would, she would listen out of sight. There were no antiques; she'd pinned up more innocuous artwork—a woven tapestry, a scenic photograph— so as, presumably, not to provoke any outlandish projections. I was sure they would come anyway, unbidden.

I wondered if she would speak, or if she would wait until I spoke first. *Why don't you tell me what brought you here today?* she might say. I had said very little in my message, just that I needed her help, and when was the soonest she could fit me in? *Would you like to tell me about your encounter with Sigmund Freud?* Of course, she wouldn't know to ask this, though it was part of the reason I had called. But I wasn't sure I was ready to talk about all that yet. I knew I wasn't. I needed to start earlier, years earlier. I needed to start at the beginning.

"The first time I came was at the opera," I said, and she didn't so much as blink, so I continued to speak.

Acknowledgments

I am grateful to the many people who helped shape this novel and who buoyed me through its creation.

Thank you to my agent, Stephanie Delman, whose determination to find this strange book a home matched my own, and who is one of the most perceptive people I have been lucky enough to know. Your support, patience, and reassurance gave me sustenance.

Thank you to my editor, Olivia Taylor Smith, whose insightful edits transformed this book. You knew just what to whittle and just where to push. Our brainstorming phone calls were clarifying, yes, but also *fun*, and I always left eager to dive back into writing. And thank you to Jaya Nicely for designing *Hysteria*'s remarkable cover and to Xiao Wang for his painting, which mesmerizes me.

Thank you to the many teachers who helped shape me into a novelist: To Gabe Hudson at Princeton, who reminded me how to play on the page. To my professors in NYU's Cultural Reporting and Criticism program: Katie Roiphe introduced me to some of the writings I hold most dear, including William Styron's *Darkness Visible*, and expanded my notion of what was possible on the page. And Susie Linfield taught me how to write—that is, how to think—with relentless clarity, and has now mentored me for close to a decade. To Beth Ann Bauman at the West Side YMCA Writer's Voice, who helped me find my way back to fiction. To my professors in The New School's MFA program, especially Helen Schulman, who interrogated my writing while also nurturing me; Darcey Steinke, who encouraged me to lean into my weirder impulses; Luis Jaramillo, whose novel-writing course was a revelation; and my adviser Katie Kitamura, whose incisive feedback transformed this book.

Thank you to my analyst, my greatest teacher.

Thank you to all those who read versions of this manuscript: To my classmates at The New School, especially Stephan Lee and my remarkable thesis group, Wynne Kontos, Nicole Cammorata, and Mike Pezley. Thanks also to Willow Belden, Alex Eggerking, and Conway Irwin for reading and brainstorming, and for buoying me.

Thank you to Josh Lambert, who led the excellent Tent: Creative Writing fellowship at the Yiddish Book Center, and to Sam Lipsyte and my cohort of fiction fellows, who offered feedback on an early version of the first chapter of this novel.

Thank you to Ruby Namdar, Ronit Muszkatblit, Elissa Strauss, and my fellows at LABA at the Fourteenth Street Y, where, far below the surface of my consciousness, this book began to germinate.

Thank you to Stephen Grosz for his writings and for speaking with me about this book at an early stage.

Thank you to the New York Public Library and to Melanie Locay, who facilitated my residencies in the Wertheim Study and the Allen Room.

Thank you to the many coffee shops I wrote in, especially the Hungarian Pastry Shop and Irving Farm on the Upper West Side.

Thank you to Anthony Venneri and Michael Panayos at the Metropolitan Opera House.

I am indebted to Peter Gay's and Joel Whitebook's biographies of Sigmund Freud and to the writings of Freud himself.

I would not have gotten through this process, or life itself, without my beloved friends. Thanks especially to Willow Belden, Ella Bennett, Nina Boutsikaris, Catherine Cushenberry, Jennifer Dolatshahi, Alex Eggerking, Miriam Gottfried, Michele Lent Hirsch, Hannah Howard, Sabine Jansen, Kyle McCarthy, Rebecca Merrill, Mike Pezley, Alice Robb, Abby Ronner, Bekah Shaughnessy, Natasja Sheriff, Jillian Steinhauer, Molly Tow, Julie Treumann, and Genevieve Walker for your conversation, laughter, and hugs.

Thank you to Matt Hunter, who nurtured me through the final phases of this process: I can hardly believe I'm lucky enough to have met you. Discovering notime with you has been one of the greatest pleasures of my life.

My family has been supportive and generous in all the ways, and I am grateful far beyond the scope of an acknowledgments section. Thank you, thank you, to my mother, Julie Gross; my father, Larry Gross; my stepmother, Jill Schuman; my grandmother, Sylvia Raynor; my brother, Andrew Gross; and my sister-in-law, Emily Ball. I love you.

About the Author

Jessica Gross's writing has appeared in the *New York Times Magazine*, *Longreads*, and the *Los Angeles Review of Books*, among other places. *Hysteria* is her first novel.